COUGAR CHRISTMAS
CATASTROPHE

TERRY SPEAR

Published by:

Wilde Ink Publishing

Cougar Christmas Catastrophe

Discover more about Terry Spear at:

http://www.terryspear.com/

Print ISBN: 978-1-63311-121-9

Ebook ISBN: 978-1-63311-201-8

SYNOPSIS

Florence Fitzgerald's world is turned upside down when she hires a new woman to work at her coffee shop in the cougar shifter-run Yuma Town and brings trouble and romance in this romantic tale of four.

Frank Everest is searching for his granddaughter, who is on the run from a stalker ex-boyfriend. He doesn't expect to meet his former coworker at the FBI or to learn that his granddaughter is working for her.

Lacy isn't about to get mixed up in the dating game while she's just trying to stay out of reach of her ex. But Rory Baker, a ranch hand at a horse ranch out of town, is eager to get to know her better.

They all have one problem—Lacy's ex-boyfriend, and the danger is very real.

I hope you all enjoy the latest Christmas tale featuring the cougars of Yuma Town, Colorado!

To Bernadette Tess Cychner, I enjoy all your Facebook comments and hope you and yours are healthy and enjoying the new year!

Florence Fitzgerald was busy making Christmas-decorated scones and pastries in the kitchen of her Fitz's Bakery and Coffee Shop while her employee, Ava Kensington, was making chicken soup on this wintry day in Yuma Town, Colorado. Florence had expanded her menu at her patrons' request.

"You're going to get an odd appeal this morning." Ava added carrots to the soup.

"Oh?" Florence wondered what that was all about, since Ava sometimes had visions of things to come. She started a fresh pot of coffee.

"Yeah. I just had a premonition that when it's time to open up the shop, you'll have an unexpected visitor."

"Who requests something of me?" Otherwise, it could be a customer.

"A young woman dressed in a knit hat, coat, and boots. I don't know what she asks about."

Florence checked the kitchen clock. "Well, it's that time." She knew Ava's premonitions would come true, just like those of Nina, her twin sister.

The shop was filled with Christmas decorations—a Christmas

tree in the window, garlands dripping with candy canes hung from shelves, cans of coffee and tea topped with red or green bows, and twinkling, colorful lights filling the windows, welcoming everyone in for treats, soups, and sandwiches. Florence loved this time of year.

The sweetness of peppermint and marshmallow, mixed with the pleasant aroma of coffee, hot chocolate, and tea, brown sugar, maple syrup, and cinnamon, drifted from behind the counter, mixing with the citrusy scent of dried orange slices strung as ornaments. Every time she entered the shop, she was overwhelmed, in a good way, by the delightful aroma of Christmas.

Florence loved the Christmas holidays and decorated to the max. The windows glimmered with rows of tiny colored bulbs, each reflecting in the glass jars lining the shelves. The wooden door framing the glass was trimmed in lights, showcasing the entryway.

She went to the door. Snow was falling, making it look magical outside. She could imagine Santa's reindeer standing on the sidewalk, peering into her shop through the big windows.

As soon as she unlocked the door and flipped the Closed sign to Open, a young woman walked up to it, dressed like Ava had said she would be. Someone Florence didn't know.

"Welcome," Florence said as she opened the door for her. "You can have a seat anywhere."

The woman was a cougar also, and she stammered, "You're a cougar...shifter."

"Yep. Ava, my assistant, is also." Florence motioned to the kitchen. "Yuma Town is cougar run."

"Oh, wow, how neat. I'm...I'm looking to get a job here. I've worked in cafés before." She pulled a resume out of her bag and handed it to Florence.

Florence closed the door to keep the cold wind out. She read over the resume. Lacy Everest. Twenty-three. She'd completed Culinary School and a Baking and Pastry School. She had worked at two different cafés, one in Orlando, Florida, and the other, a more recent one, in New Orleans, which made Florence wonder why she kept moving every few months.

Just then, three of the ranch hands working for rancher Hal Havertson, also a local part-time deputy sheriff, walked into the shop for coffee and pastries to go. They were buying for everyone out at the horse ranch, their weekly stopover when they came in for groceries and assorted other supplies for the bunkhouse.

"Welcome, boys," Florence said. "We'll have your order right up. Lacy, if you want to come with me, I'll get you started. You can hang your coat up over there on the coat rack."

"Thanks so much. You won't regret it."

Florence smiled. She would give her a chance and see how it worked out. But if Lacy's past history of employment was anything like her current, Florence suspected she wouldn't last long. Then she escorted Lacy toward the kitchen, while the guys smiled at her and tipped their cowboy hats in greeting, clearly interested in the young woman.

Florence was amused and thought they might get even more business from Hal's ranch hands now!

Lacy was a whirlwind of activity as she helped Ava and Florence package the order for the guys. Florence introduced Ava to Lacy. When Florence and Lacy carried the large order out to the ranch hands, Rory began introducing all of them to Lacy, each of the guys falling all over each other to shake her hand, smiling brightly.

"I'm Rory Baker," Rory said. "And this is Wyatt Taylor and Blaze Walker."

"I'm Lacy." She didn't offer a last name, but she appeared to be instantly attracted to Rory. Something about him seemed to draw her in, making her want to keep eye contact and challenge him.

When the guys didn't leave the shop with their fulfilled order, Lacy's cheeks reddened.

Florence said to her, "Why don't you help Ava with some of the baking?"

"Sure." Lacy looked relieved and hurried back into the kitchen.

The guys finally left, shaking their heads at each other, all of them interested in the new single cougar in town, if she were even single.

Ava was married to Chet Kensington, a Cougar Special Forces special agent who dealt with people either targeting cougars or cougar shifters, so the ranch hands had no chance with her.

"Why did you leave your other jobs?" Florence asked Lacy as she began making a peppermint-decorated cheesecake.

Lacy was making croissants and didn't say anything for a while.

Ava was finishing up an apple pie and glanced at Lacy.

"I was in an abusive relationship. I thought I had gotten away from him in Orlando, until he showed up at the café and began harassing me again. I moved to New Orleans in the middle of the night. When I finally arrived there, I got a job and thought I was safe. Then, a few weeks later, here comes Timothy. I left the job the same way I did in Orlando, slipping away from the apartment I was renting in the middle of the night. I was on my way to Denver when I saw this quaint town and your adorable coffee shop. I thought maybe a smaller town that wasn't close to any bigger city might be the way to go."

"Well, if we all get along, and you want to stay here, we'll make sure he doesn't harass you," Florence said. "Not only will all the cougars stand up for you in Yuma Town, but we have a good-sized sheriff's department and the CSF, Cougar Special Forces, special agents who live in the area and whose mission is to safeguard both cougar shifters and cougars. Ava's husband, Chet, is a CSF agent even. Is your ex-boyfriend a cougar?"

"Yeah. Timothy Wrangler is. He's a private investigator, which is how I suspect he keeps finding me. I've changed phones, not given my new address to anyone, but he always locates me."

Having a hunch it wasn't all luck, Florence called Sheriff Dan Steinacker. "I have a new employee, who just came to town, and she has a stalker ex-boyfriend. Timothy Wrangler is a private investigator. He keeps tracking her down. Can you see if she has a tracker on her car or her personal items?"

"Yeah, sure. We'll sweep all her things and see if she does."

"Okay, her name is Lacy Everest, and she's at my shop right now if you would like to talk to her."

"We'll be right over," Dan said, and then they ended the call.

"The sheriff is on his way to see if you have any tracking devices on your property."

"Oh, good, I never thought of that." Lacy sounded relieved.

"Do you have any family?"

"My parents were killed in a home invasion when I was three. My grandparents raised me, but my grandmother was shot by hunters while running with my grandfather as cougars."

"Does he know where you are?" As a retired FBI agent, Florence was used to asking lots of questions and needed to know all she could about Lacy if she was going to continue working for her and to solve the situation with Lacy's stalker.

"Uh, no. My grandfather and I are estranged."

"Oh?" Now Florence's curiosity piqued.

"Long story." Lacy didn't say anything else, and Florence, who was dying to know the truth, dropped it for now.

But she was an excellent investigator, and she would investigate it on her own if Lacy didn't tell her about it.

The door opened, and Dan, Deputy Sheriff Ricky Jones, his part-time deputy, Chase Buchanan, and Ava's husband, Chet, walked into the shop.

Florence immediately introduced Lacy to Dan and the others. Then they started sweeping her clothes and purse for trackers, found none, and went outside with her to check over her car.

Florence worried that if they did find any tracking devices,

Lacy's ex-boyfriend might already know she was here. Florence needed to learn where she was staying too, probably at one of the motels in the area for now.

She was thinking of offering Lacy a guest room in her three-bedroom home. She could stay there until she found a place. And if her ex-boyfriend came sniffing around, Florence could protect her.

"Wow," Ava said to Florence, while Lacy was outside with the officers. "That's awful about her stalker. Do you think it's true?"

"Yeah. I don't think she wanted to tell me what was going on."

"Well, this is a great place for her. Everyone will watch out for her."

Then guys and Lacy returned to the shop. "We're going to the motel where Lacy is staying and checking the rest of her clothes for bugs. She had a tracker on her car. We'll take care of it. But he might already know where she is now," Dan said.

"Once you check the rest of her property to make sure she doesn't have anything else he's tracking, she can stay with me at my house, if she wants," Florence offered. "He could know she was staying at the motel."

"Or she could stay at one of our cabins. They're closed for the winter, but since Shannon and I live right next door, I could protect her there, and it's farther from town, so he might not make the connection," Chase said.

"I'm a retired FBI agent," Florence said to Lacy. "So I'm qualified to protect you."

"Hal would put you up at the horse ranch also. He's a deputy sheriff, also, and a rancher. That would be out of town too, and he has several ranch hands and a foreman that would be there to protect you," Dan said. "Not to mention Hal would also."

"Same with us," Chet said, and gave Ava a hug and kiss before he left with the guys and Lacy.

∽

LACY NEVER IMAGINED living in a cougar-run town, but despite Mrs. Fitz's assurances that they would keep her safe, she had her doubts. Mostly because Lacy had thought she was safe before, only for Timothy to show up again and force her to run.

No one had been able to keep her safe before this. She was grateful to the shop owner for taking her in.

"I can stay with Mrs. Fitzgerald, if that would truly work for her," Lacy told the sheriff. She couldn't believe they found a tracking device in her car, but it explained how Timothy had found her so quickly.

She figured it would be a good idea to stay with someone who was law enforcement trained. If she stayed at Chase's cabin, she would be alone at night, and she could see Timothy breaking into it and putting her life in danger. If she resided at Hal's ranch, she figured the ranch hands who visited her at the shop would pressure her to date, and she was off the dating scene for now. Though they'd all been sweet. And she couldn't help but be flattered that they'd shown her all that attention.

"Okay, well, if you can do without Lacy for a little while, we'll check the rest of her property to see if tracking devices are on anything else of hers," Dan said.

"No. This needs to be done pronto. We can move your property to my house. Dan has a spare key. I have two guest bedrooms you can choose from," Florence said.

"Thanks." Lacy put on her coat and went with Dan and Chase to have her property scanned for tracking devices at the motel.

"So what brings you to Yuma Town?" Dan asked her on the way over there.

"I saw that it was a small town in the middle of nowhere on the map, and I thought Timothy wouldn't be able to locate me. Boy, did I have that wrong."

"We'll take care of you," Chase said.

"Right," Dan agreed. "You're one of us now."

She couldn't believe how everyone was so welcoming to a perfect stranger.

They arrived at the motel, all decorated in Christmas lights, with a big Christmas tree in the lobby, next to a large window, showing it off beautifully. Chet and Ricky had followed Dan there.

Dan parked, and she used her key to unlock her motel room door. She really hoped there wouldn't be any more tracking devices on her property. She worried that Timothy would already know she was stopped in Yuma Town. Not only did Ricky locate a tracking device in her luggage, but Chase found an audio listening device that could have captured conversations she'd had if Timothy had been close by.

At least it was on a bag she wasn't keeping close, so all Timothy would have heard were news reports or Christmas music on the radio when she'd been driving. She was grateful that he hadn't put one in her purse, or he would have heard her conversations if he'd been within hearing distance.

Dan made hand signals, not wanting her to speak when they found the listening device. They removed that and the tracking device.

Dan destroyed the listening device first. "A couple who ran the bank in town are driving to Denver. I'll ask if they can take the tracking devices with them. And then place them on another vehicle that has out-of-state plates. That should help to confuse your location." Then he called them and told them they would meet at the service station.

They packed Lacy's property in the trunk of Dan's hatchback and drove to the gas station to meet up with the couple.

Lacy just hoped her ex wouldn't catch up to the couple and put them in danger.

As if they understood her concern for their safety, the woman said, "I'm Yvonne Mueller and this is my husband, Rick. We're both retired FBI agents and run the bank in town now. If the ex-boyfriend harasses us, he'll wish he hadn't."

Lacy smiled, thinking she might have truly found a safe haven.

"Okay, we're off," Rick said, and they drove off with the two tracking devices in their car.

Lacy felt a bit of relief that they were going far away, but she was a little nervous about dropping off her personal belongings when they arrived at Florence's beautiful, two-story Victorian house without her being there, though the guys were all with her.

Dan said, "Her guest rooms are on the second floor, second and third bedrooms to the right at the top of the stairs. She has a master bedroom suite to the left."

"Thanks." Lacy admired the beautiful Christmas tree, decorated with a multicolored array of balls, lights, and decorations. Garlands with big red bows hung from the fireplace mantle, draped over bookcases, and the banister leading upstairs. Reindeer in brass, ceramics, and even wood were situated under miniature pine trees as if the deer had been welcomed into her miniature forest. The scent of cinnamon filled the air as Lacy noticed Christmas candles situated around the living room and kitchen.

She headed up the stairs with one of her bags while the guys carried the others behind her, and she appreciated all their help. Then they set them in the bedroom that was also decorated for Christmas. A tall, skinny Christmas tree stood in a corner of the room next to a window. The bed was covered with a quilt depicting a Christmas tree and packages. Towels were rolled up in a red wicker basket. Complimentary soaps, shampoo, toothbrush, and toothpaste were collected in another. Mrs. Fitz was truly ready for guests to stay the night.

The bedroom even had a bathroom, which she was surprised by but grateful for, giving her more privacy. Then she left the room with the guys and headed down the stairs.

"Mrs. Fitz will enjoy the company," Dan said. "I'm glad you decided to stay with her."

"Though my wife, Shannon, and I would have loved for you to stay in one of our cabins, the one closest to the main house," Chase said again. "But I agree with Dan."

"Does she often have stay-over guests?" Lacy asked. Because everything was ready for one, she wondered if she did.

"If we have a blizzard, she's prepared to open her home to anyone in need," Chase said.

"Oh, how lovely." Lacy couldn't imagine doing that, afraid she would meet dangerous people, if she did, at least with her luck.

They headed back to the shop, ordered special lattes and scones when they arrived, then wished her well, Chet giving another hug and kiss to Ava, and left.

"Your home is beautiful, and thanks so much for giving me the chance to stay there," Lacy told Mrs. Fitz.

"I'm so glad to have the company." She was all smiles, looking like she genuinely meant it. "We can decide on what we want to eat for dinner when we get home."

"Or we can make something here," Ava said.

"True. I often do that. It's easy to fix something light here and take it home for dinner," Mrs. Fitz said.

Later that afternoon, while Lacy was cleaning pots and pans, she heard one of the ranch hands had returned.

"You're back, Rory," Ava said, sounding surprised.

"Uh, yes, uh, I thought I would get one of your hot Reuben sandwiches."

"Okay, sure. So what would you like with that?"

Rory kept looking back at the kitchen.

Ava chuckled. "All right." Without waiting for him to answer, she said, "Potato chips and a pickle." Then she headed to the kitchen. "Hey, I think Rory is here to see you, Lacy."

Lacy shook her head. "I'm not dating. Not after what I've been through."

"He just wants a Reuben and chips. Ask him what he wants to drink. You'll make his day," Ava said.

"All right." Lacy didn't want to get Rory's hopes up because she really had no plan to date anyone anytime soon. What if Timothy thought she was still here, even though the tracking devices were on their way to Denver? She had stopped here. He might try to locate her—shoot, her car. Timothy could see it parked out in front of the shop. "I need to hide my car, Mrs. Fitz."

"Of course you do. I should have thought of that right away. Ava and I can't leave the shop. We're too busy this time of day, but Rory can go with you and return you here in his truck. Just park your car in the garage. Here are the keys to the house."

"Thanks so much."

"No problem. I should have thought of it when Dan and the others were here."

Lacy hated to ask Rory for help. He might feel that she wanted him for more than that, or that she was a damsel in distress, which she was, but she hated feeling that way. She left the kitchen and greeted him. "Uhm, I have a request for you if it's all right with you."

"I overheard. Sure, I'll drive over there with you and then come back for my meal."

"Thanks."

"My pleasure." He followed her in his pickup truck, and when they arrived at the house, she went inside, found the garage, opened the door, and parked her car.

Once she closed the garage door and locked up the house, she climbed into Rory's truck.

"I guess you're having a bit of trouble," he said.

"Some."

"Well, we're all here for you." Rory didn't press her to learn what it was all about, and she appreciated it.

"I can't thank everyone enough. It sure is different being in a cougar-run town."

"For sure."

When they arrived at the shop, she expected Ava to have Rory's meal ready for him, but she hadn't started it.

"I didn't want it to get cold in case there was a delay. You know how to make one, right?" Ava asked.

Lacy knew Ava was setting her up to spend more time with Rory. "Sure." Lacy got to work on the Reuben and figured that would be good for dinner tonight. It just appealed. Then she made the sandwich and added chips, realizing she should have asked him what he wanted to drink. And if he wanted this to go so he could return to the ranch to work.

"What would you like to drink?"

"Just water."

"Do you want this to go?"

"Nah, Ted, our ranch foreman, wants me to pick up some feed for the horses because we have a snowstorm on its way, and so I have more time to spare."

She hurried off to get him some water, then returned to his table with it. "Do you want anything else before I bring your meal?"

He smiled, looking like he was trying to figure out something to say, and then he finally said, "Are you free for dinner tonight?"

"Uh, no." She was, but she wasn't going to date right now while things were unresolved with her ex-boyfriend. She didn't want a new boyfriend to have to deal with him, not as volatile as Timothy could get.

Then she served up Rory's lunch, and she swore he wasn't giving up on her that easily.

After hanging around as long as he could, he popped his head in the kitchen and said goodbye, making Lacy smile. He headed out into the snow.

2

Lacy really enjoyed working with Mrs. Fitz and Ava. Both were helpful and eager to show her how they prepared their treats, while she showed them some of her own techniques.

When it was time to go to Mrs. Fitz's home, Florence said she had the ingredients for stir fry, so Lacy would have to have a Reuben another time. Stir fry sounded good.

They said goodnight to Ava, and Lacy rode home with Mrs. Fitz.

"The sheriff will share pictures of Timothy with everyone in Yuma Town. We have a private server for doing that sort of thing," Mrs. Fitz said.

"Oh, that's great. I was afraid Dan would put up some posters of him, and Timothy would realize I'm here."

"No. Dan is very discreet. But the more of us who know to be on the lookout for him, the better off you'll be. Did they find any more trackers on your property at the motel?"

"Yes. I couldn't believe it. He had placed a tracker on my suitcase and an audio listening device on a bag."

"Oh, my."

"Dan destroyed the listening device, but the tracking devices are on their way to Denver, courtesy of Yvonne and Rick Mueller," Lacy said.

"They're good folk. They'll be sure to leave them somewhere that will throw your ex-boyfriend off your trail."

"I sure hope so."

It was getting dark out, and Christmas lights twinkled on all the homes they passed. It made it look like a Christmas town. Not one house was unadorned.

"I love all the Christmas lights."

"Oh, yes. We have contests, and anyone who can't manage to put up their own lights has fellow cougars hang them up. We just buy our own lights."

When they reached Mrs. Fitz's home, Lacy loved the icicle lights hanging off the roof and first-story windows, and the white lights covering the trees.

"Beautiful," Lacy said.

"Thanks. I love the holiday festivities."

Lacy had pretty much kept to herself and hadn't participated in holiday fun for the last couple of years, mainly because of dating Timothy, who hated the holidays because of his dysfunctional family—so he said. He had never told her anything about them, even when she asked.

She liked the holiday atmosphere—the decorations, caroling, parties—but he had avoided all that nonsense, his words, and hadn't liked it when she decorated for the holidays.

Even when the café she had worked at held a Christmas party for employees and their families, he didn't want her to attend, and he wouldn't go either. But she did. She wasn't about to forgo the one party she got to go to a year, which made him furious. She'd tried to break up with him after that, without success.

"We have a big Christmas dance coming up next weekend and a Christmas bazaar where cougars sell their crafts and treats for Christmas," Mrs. Fitz said.

"Oh, how fun."

"We have Santa visit with the ladies in town at a special event, the proceeds going to our library."

Lacy smiled. "I feel like I'm in Santa's Village."

"We love the holidays, but we also love the camaraderie. We have several community events throughout the year."

Inside the house, Mrs. Fitz turned on her Christmas tree lights and strings of lights on the mantle and on the banister, covered in garland, and red and green plaid bows.

Then they went into the kitchen and worked together to make stir-fry sugar snap peas, miniature corn on the cob, bell pepper slices, and onions. Mrs. Fitz cut up strips of steak to add to the pan.

"You can't know how much I enjoy your company and that you're a cook who can help out in the kitchen." Mrs. Fitz added seasoning to the pan.

"Yeah, this is fun. My ex-boyfriend didn't cook so it's fun to share tips in cooking with a fellow chef."

Then they sat down to eat, and Mrs. Fitz asked, "You really don't want to let your grandfather know where you are?"

"I blame him for my grandmother's death." Lacy didn't want to talk about it. But since she was Mrs. Fitz's guest, she figured she might as well get it out in the open.

"Oh?" Mrs. Fitz took another bite of her stir-fry.

Lacy sighed. "They went on a cougar run. Three hunters shot my grandmother, and my grandfather hid."

"As a cougar, he couldn't have fought three armed hunters," Mrs. Fitz said. "They would have killed him too."

Deep down, Lacy knew that. But she had wanted her grandfather to kill the hunters so badly for what they had done that she couldn't see past her upset. Her grandmother and grandfather had raised her from a toddler, and she couldn't see not having her grandmother around any longer.

"Just like if the roles had been reversed, if the hunters had shot your grandfather, your grandmother couldn't have fought them without getting herself killed. Neither would have wanted that to happen to their mate."

Lacy moved her food around on her plate.

"Your grandmother must have turned into her human form at death."

"She did. The hunters had finally reached her body and were in shock that the cougar they thought they had shot had turned into a naked woman. They buried her with leaves, and my grandfather pursued them then. He followed them to their camp, where they hurriedly broke it down, loaded it into a pickup, and took off. He should have killed them then."

"Did he report it to the police?"

"Yes. He returned to his clothes, shifted, dressed, and called 911. He also set her clothes nearby. He couldn't dress her, or he wouldn't be able to explain that the bullets hadn't gone through her clothes or that she didn't have blood on them."

"He was smart to do that." Mrs. Fitz drank some of her water.

"He's a retired FBI agent. But yeah, I guess anyone could have figured that he couldn't dress her."

"Then the police arrived and...?"

"They thought my grandfather had shot her. You know how it goes. Family members closest to the victim are always suspected of committing the crime. He found the body. He was the one at the scene of the crime."

"Sure."

"He told them about the hunters, but they were long gone."

"But they left behind shell casings? And a sign of a camp—fire-wood, the place where the tents had been set up, footprints, tire tracks?"

"Yes. They did check Granddad's car to see if he had rifles in it, but he didn't. His shoes and tire tracks didn't match the ones at the camp. And they saw there had been three men's boot imprints at the camp. They checked Granddad's hands for gunpowder residue, and he didn't have any. Then they had police officers track down the license plate of the truck the hunters drove off in."

"And they had rifles."

"And gun powder residue on their hands. When the police investigators tested the weapons to determine if they were the same ones that had been used to kill my grandmother, they found they were. The hunters swore up and down that they had killed a cougar that had been stalking them."

"As a shifter, she wouldn't have been stalking them," Mrs. Fitzgerald.

"Right. She wasn't. They hunted her down just because she was a cougar."

"So your grandfather had done the right thing in letting the police handle it."

Lacy let out her breath. "They went to prison for forty years. But those men should have been dead."

"I agree. But if he had killed them as a cougar, they would have hunted any cougar down in the area."

"Yeah. You're right."

"So do you want to tell your grandfather where you are?" Mrs. Fitz ate the rest of her dinner.

Lacy began working on hers again.

She wasn't sure if she wanted to, but she could imagine he was worried sick about her.

"Did he know you were having trouble with the cougar in an abusive relationship?"

"He told me when I was first dating Timothy that he was bad news. I...I didn't listen to my grandfather."

"So he could be worried about you when you went missing without a word."

Lacy sighed. "Yeah. You're right. Knowing my grandfather, he has half his FBI agent friends who are still working at the agency looking for me. I didn't think of that."

She pulled out her phone and called her grandfather, afraid a text message wouldn't cut it. He could think her ex-boyfriend was sending it or coercing her to send it.

Her grandfather answered right away. "Lacy, are you all right?"

"Yes, Granddad. I'm living in a cougar-run town, have a job at a coffee shop, and am staying with the shop's owner for now until I get a place of my own."

"Who is the man you're staying with?"

She was amused that he thought it was a man and was probably worried about her hooking up with someone older.

"Florence Fitzgerald, Granddad. Not a man. She's a retired—"

"FBI agent," her granddad said, sounding surprised.

She frowned and looked at Mrs. Fitz. "You know her?"

"Yeah, we worked on several assignments together."

"Oh. So I guess you know that I'm safe then."

"Where?"

"Yuma Town, Colorado. The whole town has offered to protect me, so you don't have to worry about me."

"I'll be there as soon as I can."

"You don't have to do that."

"See you soon. Love you." Then he hung up.

"Great." Lacy finished her dinner.

"I'm glad you called him."

"Yeah, but now he's coming here to protect me. So you know him?"

"Frank Everest? Yeah. We often didn't agree on cases."

"So you didn't date him?"

Florence laughed. "No, dear. We were both married at the time. I wouldn't have dated him for anything even if we hadn't been married."

Lacy laughed. She felt more lighthearted than she had in

months. She was glad she was here. She never expected to hear anyone say that about her grandfather. Almost everyone really liked him, and she wondered what the beef had been between the two FBI agents on the cases.

"Ready for some dessert?" Mrs. Fitz was going to take their empty dishes into the kitchen, but Lacy quickly did the honors.

"Yeah, sure."

"Sugar cookie cheesecake bars?" Mrs. Fitz brought out the Christmas tree dessert plates and then added the cheesecake bars, covered in red and green sprinkles shaped like Christmas trees.

"Hmm, that looks good. I love cheesecake. That's something I need to make for the holidays. I never thought of having little cheesecake squares decorated for Christmas."

"I love cheesecake and had to figure out a way to include it for the holidays."

"This has been so much fun. Thanks so much for allowing me to stay with you and work for you."

"I'm glad to do it."

After eating dessert and cleaning up, they headed to bed.

Despite feeling relatively safe at Mrs. Fitz's house, after Lacy took her shower, she shifted into her cougar and slept on top of the comforter in her furry form—just in case they had a break-in.

"Hey, Rory, we didn't expect you to return to the ranch that soon after you went in to have a meal and pick up supplies," Wyatt said as Rory retired to the bunkhouse with the other ranch hands for the night.

"Yeah, we figured you might even take Lacy to a movie," Blaze said. "Did she turn you down?"

Rory knew he should have stayed in Yuma Town longer, to make it look like he'd had a date with her so the other guys wouldn't immediately go after her. "She was having dinner with Mrs. Fitz since she'd been so gracious to hire her and let her stay with her at her home."

"Yeah, sure," Blaze said, laughing.

"I'm telling Ted I'm picking up supplies for the ranch next time," Wyatt said.

Rory had to make sure he got to see her first! But he didn't want to make her feel they were obsessing over her, even though they all wanted to see more of her. He realized he didn't even have her telephone number, so he could message her.

It was getting really late when he got a call from Mrs. Fitz, and since he never got calls from her, he figured something was wrong. "Hi, Mrs. Fitz. What's up?"

"Lacy has gone to bed, but I just wanted to tell you, and you can share with the other fellas that she has had a stalker ex-boyfriend following her. I know you all want to date her, but just keep in mind that she might be a little shy about it until she feels more comfortable with her surroundings."

"Oh, yeah, of course." So that changed everything for him, and for the other guys too as far as pursuing her.

"You might not have checked the cougar site, but Dan posted the picture of her ex. If you see him, be sure to report it to the sheriff's office."

"Hell, yeah. Thanks for letting me know." He rarely looked at the site.

"Okay, I'm going to let you go, but I just wanted you and the others to know that she might need a little time to get in the mood for dating."

"For sure. Thanks." When they ended the call, Wyatt was coming out of one of the bathrooms after having a shower. Rory mentioned the situation with Lacy's ex-boyfriend to him. Then he pulled up the site and saw the man who had been harassing Lacy. "Here he is."

Blaze came out of his bedroom and looked at the site. "Well, hell. I wonder how long it will take before she feels comfortable dating."

But Rory wasn't giving up on getting to know her. He would offer to be a sounding board for her and not push her into dating until she was ready, if ever. He just hoped Blaze and Wyatt wouldn't try to meet up with her while he was trying to make some headway.

He looked at the photo of her ex, blond-haired and bearded, with icy blue eyes, a square jaw, and an unsmiling expression. He appeared hard and unyielding. Rory wondered why Lacy would have dated the guy. But maybe he'd been charming and sweet with her in the beginning. He really wanted to know what had gone wrong with their relationship. And what had happened after they ended it.

Bright and early the next morning, Rory said to Ted, their foreman, "Hey, boss, it's Friday."

"Do you want me to get our special treats from Mrs. Fitz's shop?"

"Yeah. If that works for you."

Usually, the guys switched off on who made the Friday rounds, but since Rory had gone into town again yesterday, he was afraid Ted would send one of the other ranch hands to do the job.

Ted smiled. "You're the first one who asked, so sure. It wouldn't happen to be because you want to see the little filly now working at the shop, would it?"

Rory chuckled. "Yeah. I'm off to see what everyone wants, and I'm out of here." Usually, he would call it in and then just pick it up, but he wanted the time to stay there and really see if he could make some headway with Lacy.

"All right. See you when we see you."

That's what Rory loved about working at Hal's ranch. Everyone in the family treated the ranch hands as family. And Ted was the same way as their foreman.

Once Rory had the list of treats on his phone, he drove off to Yuma Town, hoping he wouldn't screw this up with Lacy. Maybe she would like to run as a cougar with him, even if she didn't want to date.

3

L acy was busy making scones when she heard the bell jingle on the coffee shop door, and Mrs. Fitz glanced out from the kitchen and said, "I'll cover for you, Lacy. You take care of the customer."

"Sure." When Lacy left the kitchen, she was surprised to see Rory smiling back at her, tipping his cowboy hat in greeting, his smile contagious. He was just charming in his cowboy duds and a light, coffee-colored suede jacket lined with fleece. He looked huggable, when she should have been scolding herself for any such thoughts after the last boyfriend disaster.

"Morning," Rory said, hanging his jacket up on one of the hooks on the wall for patrons' jackets and coats.

"Morning. What will you have?"

"I have a list of what everyone wants at the ranch, but I'll get something here. How about a grilled cheese and ham croissant? And a cup of coffee."

"Sure. Coming right up." Lacy returned to the kitchen, amused, knowing Rory was trying to get on her good side. Then she thought about the Christmas dance this weekend. She would love to have a date for it.

When she made up his croissant, she took it and the cup of coffee out to him. "Do you dance?"

"I sure do. I love to dance."

"Will you take me to the Christmas dance?"

His face lit up like a Christmas tree. He was really cute. "Yes, ma'am. I sure will."

"Perfect."

"Do you want to go out to dinner tonight?" Rory wasn't giving up on her.

Then again, she had given him an opening to ask her when she asked him to take her to the dance. Even though she'd had trouble with her ex-boyfriend, it didn't mean any other guy she met would be anything like him.

"Sure."

"What appeals? Mexican food? We have Jose's Taco Shop. Or pizza at The Sizzling Slice?"

"Either sounds good." She thought about it for a moment more. "Let's have Mexican food."

"All right. I'll pick you up at six at Mrs. Fitz's home?"

"Yeah, that would work."

"All right. Super." He sounded thrilled.

She still felt it was a little sudden to date someone else, but he truly appealed to her. Not only was he charming, but he was also physically beautiful, with a chiseled face and a dark-colored, light beard. He was dark-haired, his bangs flopping over to his right side, and his hair wavy, not cut short. He had the most disarming brown eyes, and his lips looked perfectly kissable.

After he ate his breakfast, he gave her the list of all the breakfast food the Havertons, ranch hands, and their foreman and his mate had ordered. Then Chase entered the shop and ordered breakfast for the sheriff's department, their usual treat on Friday mornings also.

"Hey, Rory," Chase said.

"Hey, Chase."

Chase said to Lacy, "We haven't had any sightings of your ex-boyfriend, and the Muellers dropped off the trackers in a pickup truck heading out of Denver toward Nevada, though the vehicle had a Utah plate, so he might be heading further west and going home."

"That's good news."

"We're still watching for Timothy in case he realizes we pulled a fast one on him."

"Good. Because he's clever."

"That's why we're prepared in case he does something unexpected and learns somehow that you're here. But he won't get the welcome he might expect," Chase said.

"That's great. Maybe he'll get the message then." Lacy gave Rory the order for the ranch and said, "I'll see you tonight."

Chase raised an eyebrow at Rory. He smiled sheepishly. "See you tonight, Lacy." He tipped his hat, grabbed his jacket, slipped into it, and headed out the door.

Ava finished filling Chase's order and handed it to him. "Thanks, Ava."

"My pleasure."

Then Chase took off.

"By tomorrow, everyone will know that you are going on a date with Rory *and* going to the dance with him," Mrs. Fitz said, smiling, as she made sourdough loaves of bread.

"Because Chase will spread the word?"

"Rory will. Chase didn't know you were going to the dance with Rory. But Rory will want every bachelor cougar in Yuma Town know you're going to it with him so that you don't get asked over and over again," Mrs. Fitz said.

Then they heard the door ding again, and more customers came in to order or pick up breakfasts.

By the time they closed the shop that evening, Lacy was looking forward to having dinner with Rory.

She changed at Mrs. Fitz's house into a wool skirt, sweater, and boots, nice and warm, casual dressy. Then Rory arrived early, and she was glad she was already there. She was famished.

"I thought we could go to the Watering Hole afterward, if you want. Though Jose's Taco Shop has cocktails too and desserts."

"Let's just see how we feel after dinner."

"Okay, that sounds good." Then he took her in his new pickup truck. It was an aqua color, and she loved the uniqueness.

"Have you been in Jose's Taco Shop yet?"

"No, I haven't even seen it," she said.

"It's really a swell restaurant. Great atmosphere, and the food and service are terrific."

"Oh, good. It's awful to go to a place that has great ambience, but the food isn't great."

"You'll love it. They even have rib-eye steak fajitas."

"Oh, now that sounds good."

"They're out of this world."

"So what did the other guys say about you going out to dinner with me?" She knew he had told them that he was.

Rory chuckled. "We were told about your ex-boyfriend stalker and that you might not want to go out with anyone for a while after that trauma in your life. So when I told them I was going out to dinner with you and taking you to the Christmas dance, I got a couple of slaps on the back in good humor. They said they knew I was up to no good when I got to Ted first and asked to pick up our Friday morning breakfasts."

She smiled. "I have to admit that once the Muellers said they would take the trackers to Denver, I was feeling more comfortable about getting on with my life. Still, I was afraid that if I started dating anyone, even if it was just short-term, and Timothy learned of it, the guy I was dating would be in just as much danger as I've been."

"I would have taken care of the menace." Rory sounded serious, and she figured he would have confronted Timothy, but who knew how her ex would react. Badly, she was certain, unless he was only a menace to women and couldn't deal with a man confronting him.

When they arrived at the restaurant, she loved the exterior. Tile porch, orange walls, blue doors, a water fountain, though turned off now for winter weather. For the seating outside, all the chairs were painted in different colors. Rounded arches were painted orange, with pink trim. It was delightful. Then they parked and went inside the restaurant.

A bar was covered in pretty Mexican tile, and murals of charros on horseback and women dressed in colorfully embroidered traditional shirts and skirts were painted on the walls. Sombreros lined the wall above them. Spanish music played in the background.

Water tumbled down a fountain wall, making her feel as though she was outside enjoying the pleasant sound of a waterfall. A glowing fire in the fireplace warmed the room. A Christmas tree sporting red chili peppers, red bows, and red and green Christmas lights was tucked into one corner of the room. They were seated in a booth, and she loved the atmosphere. Most of the tables were taken, indicating the restaurant's popularity.

Several people smiled and acknowledged them. She wasn't used to going into a restaurant where everyone was so friendly. They probably all knew Rory and were curious about her.

They ended up ordering the rib-eye fajitas for two.

She had expected a little taco shack, so she was really impressed by the place's beauty. She was glad she had suggested coming here.

Once they had their margaritas, hers with sugar on the rim, his with salt, they toasted to a delightful dinner and new beginnings. Their fajitas were served, and they began eating them.

"Ohmigosh, these are so tender and delicious." She had never had such tender meat in a fajita before, and she knew where she would come for her fajitas from now on.

"Yeah, when they began serving them like this, though they have the cheaper cuts also that are more affordable, the guys and I began ordering the rib-eye fajitas."

"I can see why. So are you from Colorado, born and bred?"

"Yeah. I came from Breckinridge. Though I love skiing, I love working on a horse ranch in a cougar-run town even better. Speaking of cougars, do you want to run as big cats after dinner?"

"Oh, sure, I would love to. I couldn't run as a cougar where I was living before."

"Well, we can run anywhere out here. We have strict no-hunting laws in the area. Not that we don't have issues with hunters from time to time, thinking that the rules don't apply to them, but for the most part, we're safe."

"That would be great."

"At some time, I'll drive you out to the ranch, and we can run out there. But I'll take you in the woods here this time, where it's closer to town."

"Okay, perfect." She called Mrs. Fitz, just to let her know she might be coming in a little later because they were going running as cougars after dinner.

"Oh, my, that sounds like fun."

"Do you want to go with us?" Lacy wondered if Mrs. Fitz ever got out to run with other cougars.

"Oh, no, dear. You two have fun."

"Thanks. The food is incredible here at Jose's Taco Shop."

"I love their rib-eye fajitas."

Lacy laughed. "That's what we're enjoying now. Okay, before my date thinks I've abandoned him, I'll let you go."

"Have a great time."

"Thanks!" Lacy *was* having a great time.

"Is Mrs. Fitz coming running with us?" Rory sounded just fine with it, which Lacy appreciated.

Her ex wouldn't have been. Timothy didn't want her to have any friends of her own and tried to cut her off from them. But she hadn't allowed it. That had made him angry and impossible to live with.

"She declined my offer. My ex would have been furious if he had been sitting in your place and I had suggested it."

"I thought it was nice for you to include her. We would have had fun as a threesome."

"I didn't want her to feel left out in case she doesn't get out as a cougar very often to run and explore. But I appreciated how nice you were about it. My ex-boyfriend was really controlling and didn't want me to have any friends anymore. Just him. I only have my grandfather, and he didn't want me to talk to him either, though we were estranged and I wasn't in touch with him anyway."

"I'm sorry to hear it. I don't have any family left, so the Havertons and their hired help have become family. I once dated a woman who was terribly controlling. She didn't want me to speak with my friends at the Watering Hole; all my attention had to be paid to her. She finally left town before I called it quits with her, which I fully intended to do that morning. The guys all hassled me mercilessly for putting up with her for so long."

"Oh, I know what you mean. I felt the same way. All my friends kept telling me to ditch him, but when I did, he wasn't going for it. I kept hoping he would find someone else to hassle, not that I really wished him on anyone else, but I just wanted him to leave me alone. I finally left the state, but when he followed me there, I knew I was in trouble. Did you ever hear from your ex-girlfriend?"

"No. Once she was gone, I never knew what had happened to her and didn't want to. We have such a great community here; we don't need anyone like her living here."

"You weren't afraid I would be like that?"

"Nope. And then when I heard your story, I realized you really weren't like her in any way. Instead, you are more like me, having to deal with a controlling, aggressive person, except I was lucky that she just took off, and that was the end of that."

After they finished their fajitas and had sopapillas for dessert, Rory paid for dinner, and he drove her to a hiking trail and parked at the trailhead.

"Do you want to strip here at the truck or change in the woods?" Rory asked.

"Let's change in the truck. It'll be warmer. I'll use the back seat."

"I'll do it after you do."

With the ground covered in snow, it would definitely be the warmer option. She moved to the back seat, stripped off her clothes, and then shifted. Rory came around to the back door, let her out, then climbed in, left the door open, and removed his clothes. He shifted and leapt out of the truck. She shut the door with her paws.

Then he nuzzled her with a sweet rub of his muzzle, their whiskers tickling each other, greeting her cougar to cougar as a sign of trust, and she nuzzled him back, enjoying the intimacy. Then he took off to show her the way. They were on the trail, and then off the trail, leaving their paw prints in the snow. She was glad that the area was off-limits to hunters, or they would be easy to track.

The snow was falling in fat flakes, adding to the already covered pine branches and Colorado spruce. She loved it. She had lived in Florida, where there was no snow, and it was really fun to run through the snow in Colorado. Everything looked Christmas card perfect.

Rory got ahead of her, and she nipped at his tail in fun. He rounded on her and tried to tackle her to the ground, but she retaliated with her paws up, claws sheathed, and teeth bared in playful big cat fun.

He snarled at her, and she copied his stance, the two trying to bite each other's neck, but their teeth clashed instead. Then they dropped down, their hearts beating like crazy, their breaths smoking in the freezing air. Then they licked each other on the muzzle. This was great.

She'd never played with a cougar like that. He was so gentle with her. She wouldn't have dared to try that with her ex. Then they continued exploring the woods when they came to a clearing.

As soon as they walked into the clearing covered in snow, they saw a bull moose. Ohmigod, she had never seen one in person. He was dark brown with huge antlers. He was about six feet tall at the shoulder, and she knew they weighed about a half-ton. They could be dangerous if he spied them and felt they were a threat.

Which, since they were cougars right now, they sure could be. Then he charged them. A moose could run 35 miles per hour at short distances. She and Rory headed for the woods, though he stayed behind her as if to protect her. She leapt into the lower branches of a tree and began climbing. Rory was right behind her as the moose stopped before ramming into the tree.

Then he grazed on the needles of the pine tree way below them. They weren't going anywhere for a while. Though they could run 40-50 miles per hour as cougars, they figured they would just wait out the moose and then return to the truck. At least she was fine with it. If Rory indicated he wanted to leave sooner, she would stick with him.

They watched the moose for a while, then he finally wandered off the way he had come. They still waited until he was some distance off. Then Lacy zigzagged down the tree, landing on branch after branch on her descent, knocking off snow, creating a sudden snowstorm. Rory moved down at the same pace on branches close by, appearing to want to reach the base of the tree trunk at the same time as her, protective, endearing.

When they landed on the ground in a pile of snow, they looked back in the direction of the moose. He had paused and turned his head to consider them. They tore off, leaping through mounded snow. Lacy glanced over her shoulder and saw Rory peering back. The moose had sauntered off.

They were safe. They nuzzled each other and headed to the trailhead that took them another half hour of trekking through the snow to reach. Despite the momentary terror of the moose charging after them, and that had been an experience and a half, making it memorable, though, she had had a blast with Rory.

He shifted next to the truck, let her in, closed the door, then shifted back, waiting in the snow as a cougar for her to dress. As soon as she had, she opened the door for him, and he jumped into the back seat and licked her cheek with his sandpapery tongue. She wrapped her arms around his neck and hugged him. Then she left the truck and returned to the front passenger seat.

He soon joined her in the driver's seat and smiled at her. "What did you think about that adventure?"

She laughed. "I loved seeing the moose. I have to say that it's the first time I've been a cougar in the snow, and I really enjoyed it. But being chased by a moose? What a fantastic memory."

He smiled. "I'm glad you weren't terrified."

"Momentarily. He was big and running fast. I figured that we might have outrun the moose. I know that, as a human, if you hide behind a tree, they don't see you, and the threat is gone to them, so they'll usually just stop. But for us, climbing the tree was perfect. We could have outrun him too, but if he followed us to the truck, then what? We would stop to get into the truck and would have been in danger. He could have struck us. So waiting in the tree was the right thing to do."

"I agree. I can't believe I took you on a fun-filled cougar run and we had to get out of the way of a raging bull."

She laughed. "We'll remember it forever." She didn't mean as in she was mating him, but just as a life experience.

"For sure." He drove her to Mrs. Fitz's home and parked.

Lacy leaned over the console and kissed him. "Thanks for a delightful dinner and run as cougars. It was just perfect, and I had the best time ever."

Rory kissed her back, rubbing her shoulders with his hands in a soothing massage. "Do you want to have dinner at the Sizzling Slice tomorrow night?"

She laughed. "And a cougar run afterward?"

"I'll take you out to the ranch. We can run up into the rocky hills if we have trouble."

"Okay, sounds good."

Then he walked her to the house, pulled her into a hug, and kissed her again. She wrapped her arms around his neck, kissing him deeper. Yeah, being with Rory felt just right.

She was already thinking about going further with him, which was probably crazy, but she hadn't had intimate relations with her ex in six months. With Rory, she just wanted to go further. But he lived in a bunkhouse, and she was staying with Mrs. Fitz, so it seemed privacy would be impossible.

"I'll see you tomorrow then." Rory rubbed her arms and then kissed her forehead in a really tender way.

She smiled. "Sounds great."

The day after that was the Christmas dance so she needed to figure out what to wear for it. When she entered the house, Mrs. Fitz was reading a book on the couch and drinking hot cocoa. "Did you have a good time?"

"We encountered a moose and ended up in a tree." Lacy laughed. "I've never seen one for real. Boy, was he huge. But yeah, we had a great time. We're going out to dinner tomorrow night." She had to tell Mrs. Fitz so she wouldn't expect to have dinner with her.

"And the dance."

"I'm going with Rory."

"Oh, wonderful."

Lacy wanted to know if Mrs. Fitz was going too, but she didn't want to make her feel bad if she didn't have anyone to go with and wasn't attending because of it.

"Would you like some hot cocoa?"

"No thanks. It's late. I'm going to take a shower and head to bed." They had to get up so early to start preparing breakfast dishes at the coffee shop that Lacy was tired.

"Okay. See you in the morning."

All Lacy could think about was enjoying her time with Rory tomorrow at dinner and looking forward to another fun-filled run.

FLORENCE WAS SO glad Lacy was having such a good time with Rory. He was a great guy—the same with the other ranch hands. Lacy needed someone in her life to prove to her that good men existed in the world, not like her ex-boyfriend.

Florence had just about fallen asleep when she heard a knock on the front door.

She frowned, threw on some clothes, and grabbed her gun from her bedside table. She called Dan next as she headed down the stairs. "I've got an unexpected visitor. I'm going to check it out, taking my gun, but I just wanted to let you know in case I have trouble."

"I'm on my way. If it's Lacy's ex-boyfriend, don't open the door."

4

————

Florence reached her front door and opened the wooden speakeasy door to look out, and was shocked to see that it was Frank Everest, Lacy's grandfather. She was still on the phone with Dan and said, "It's just Lacy's grandfather. We're good."

"Are you sure?"

"Yeah, I worked with him in the FBI."

"All right. If you have any trouble, just let me know."

"I will. Thanks." Mrs. Fitz closed the speakeasy window and opened the door. "Come in, and I'll make us some cocoa. Lacy's sleeping upstairs. Do you have a place to stay?"

"I'm staying at the motel in Yuma Town. I'm good, but cocoa sounds great."

She hadn't seen Frank in twenty years, but he looked so distinguished with his silver hair, blue eyes, and his kindly features. He gave her a warm smile, though their relationship while working together on cases in the FBI had often been contentious. They both had their own way of doing things and never agreed. But somehow, they always solved their cases.

He removed his hat, scarf, and coat, then joined her in the kitchen.

He smelled of snow and fresh air, and she recognized his cougar's scent right away.

"Has Lacy's ex been spotted in town?"

"Not yet. I was afraid you might have been him." Florence pulled her gun out of her pocket and put it on the kitchen counter.

He chuckled. "That's the Florence I remember."

"Yeah, I'm always prepared." She poured the cocoa into snowman mugs, topped them with whipped cream and peppermint pieces, and then handed one to Frank.

They moved into the living room to get comfortable.

"Okay, so the situation is that the sheriff's department found tracking devices on Lacy's car and bag, and they arranged to have them taken to Denver, and left the trackers in a truck heading out of state."

"Well, hell, no wonder he kept locating her. Did she tell you why we were estranged?"

"Yeah. I think I convinced her that you really had no choice with regard to your wife, her grandmother's death."

"Thanks. I couldn't seem to get through to her about it."

"I think she was just in denial that you could have done more for your wife."

"I agree."

"In any case, I'm sorry to hear that she died. If you hadn't guessed, Yuma Town is cougar run. We take care of our own. So everyone in town has been alerted about her ex-boyfriend and is on the lookout for him."

"That's a relief," Frank said. "I smelled a man had been at the house."

"Oh, Rory Baker. He's a ranch hand at Hal Haverton's horse ranch. Hal's also a part-time deputy sheriff. Rory took Lacy out to dinner tonight. He's a good guy. You don't have to worry about him being like her ex-boyfriend."

"Good. How are you doing?"

"Wonderfully. I retired and ended up in Yuma Town, started my coffee shop, and love it here. You?"

"Like you, I retired, lost my wife to hunters, and lost Lacy over that. But when she began having issues with the ex-boyfriend, I had tried to protect her, but she wasn't having anything to do with it. You can't know how worried I have been about her safety. I had looked into Timothy and discovered he'd done the same thing with two previous girlfriends until he ended up with another girlfriend."

"And you couldn't have him arrested if he hurt Lacy because he's a shifter."

"Exactly."

"How long do you plan to stay?"

"For a couple of weeks to see how Lacy is doing and try to rekindle our relationship."

"That sounds like a great idea." She was going to offer her home to him if he would be more comfortable there, but she would wait to see if things worked out between him and his granddaughter in a few days.

"When does she go to work in the morning?"

"Five. But you can come by any time to see her. You can take her out to lunch. She has a dinner date with Rory again tomorrow night and for a cougar run. So she might be in late like she was tonight."

"Okay, well, I'll let you get some sleep. I'll drop by the shop for breakfast in the morning."

"All right. We'll see you then."

He took his snowman mug into the kitchen, and she deposited both in the dishwasher. Then he said good night, and she locked up afterwards. She was glad the visitor at her door had been Lacy's grandfather and hoped Lacy and her grandfather would resolve their differences.

And she hoped Lacy wouldn't be annoyed with her for telling her grandfather she was dating Rory!

Then she had a weird thought. If Lacy's grandfather was going to be here for the holidays, would he want to go to the Christmas dance with her? Not to dance, but just as company? The same with Christmas Eve dinner and Christmas Day meals.

No way would she let him stay in the motel for the holidays while he was trying to make up to Lacy to change her view of him.

Florence returned to bed, and it wasn't long before it was time to get up and make breakfast, but Lacy was already working on it. "Is French toast all right?" she asked Florence with a cheerful smile.

"Oh, sure, that's great. You probably smelled your grandfather's scent in the house."

"I did. I knew he would be here before long."

"He's staying at the motel. I told him you were sleeping, and he said he would be here for a couple of weeks."

Lacy nodded. "It's probably a good thing that we iron things out."

"Especially before the holidays. About that, since you're both here, how do you feel about him coming to Christmas Eve and Christmas Day meals?"

"That would be great. Maybe Rory can join us."

"I did tell Frank that you and Rory are going out to dinner tonight, but that he can come to the shop at any time to talk to you." Florence poured cups of coffee for both of them and brought the cream and sugar to the table.

Lacy didn't say anything for the moment, then served up their French toast and a side of bacon.

When they sat down to eat, Lacy asked, "Are you going to the Christmas dance?"

"Sure. I go every year. There's always someone to dance with, even if they are much, much younger than me."

Lacy laughed. "Okay. I was afraid to ask you about it."

"Yeah, and we have a girls-only fundraiser with a sexy Santa tea party."

"Oh, how fun."

"It is. One of the bachelors dresses up as Santa. We'll be making the desserts for the fundraiser, and we'll take pictures with Santa."

"What about my grandfather? Can he go to the dance?"

"Absolutely. While he's staying here, he can join in all the holiday events."

They started eating their breakfast.

"This is really good. Thanks for making it," Florence said.

"Thanks. I never make it for myself. But for a couple of us, I thought it would be fun to make it. So, are you considering letting my grandfather stay at your house also?"

"It's something that could happen, if both of you would like. I have another spare guest room. It's up to the two of you."

Lacy sighed. "I could spend more time with him at your house, if it would be all right with you, and he might not feel as lonely, if we're all watching a movie together or spending time having dinner together."

"But you're going out with Rory." Florence assumed Lacy would continue dating Rory at night, taking breaks occasionally. But Florence would end up being the one to have dinner with Frank instead. Otherwise, he would have to go out every night to get something to eat, since the motel didn't have a restaurant.

"I'll ask him if he drops by the coffee shop today." Lacy finished her breakfast and carried her plate into the kitchen. Then she cleaned up the pots and pans.

Florence soon joined her and put the dishes away. "Are you ready to go to the shop?"

"Yep. Thanks for talking me into letting my grandfather know where I was. I'm eager to work things out between us."

"Good. It's hard when it's the holidays, and you don't have any family to connect with."

Lacy looked regretful that she had treated her grandfather with disdain when he had been so adamant about protecting her from her ex-boyfriend, even though she had not really been ready to admit she had an issue with Timothy.

Then they headed to the shop. Before they even entered it, Frank was at the door, waiting for them to open up shop. Florence smiled at him. "Are you hungry? Come in and Lacy can get you something."

Just then, Ava arrived, greeted them, and headed back to the kitchen. Florence joined her.

THEN MRS. FITZ and Ava began baking, and Lacy handed her grandfather a menu and got him a cup of coffee. "Uhm, Mrs. Fitz said you could stay with us at the house, if you would like. I would love it if you would. I could visit with you at night, when I'm not out on dates with Rory. Mrs. Fitz has another spare bedroom." Then she leaned over and whispered, "When I'm not at home, you can keep Mrs. Fitz company. She's lonely."

Her grandfather smiled. She didn't know how it would go between her grandfather and Mrs. Fitz since they had been adversaries when they worked on cases together. But maybe they would like the companionship.

"That would be nice."

"And you can ask her to the Christmas dance."

He raised his brows, his lips smiling.

"Rory and I are going together. I asked him. Mrs. Fitz said she always goes. But I thought if you stayed with us, you could take her."

Again, he smiled. "Sure, Lacy. I'll ask her."

"Okay. Do you know what you want?"

"The cinnamon roll."

"Coming right up." Then she whipped around, went into the kitchen, and found Ava working on cinnamon rolls.

"One of our best sellers," Ava said.

"That's what my grandfather wants," Lacy said.

"I'm glad he has come for the holidays," Ava said.

"I agree." Lacy turned to Mrs. Fitz. "Granddad agreed to stay with us."

"Wonderful. That would be great."

Lacy didn't tell her that he would ask her to go to the dance. That was between her grandfather and Mrs. Fitz.

FRANK WAS glad to have the offer to stay at Florence's home for the holidays. It would make it so much easier to visit with his granddaughter. But also, he wanted to get to know Florence better—not as agents working cases, but maybe even dating. He would be happy to take her to the Christmas dance if she wanted him to.

Once his wife had died, he hadn't dated afterward. But he did know Florence, and he liked that they did have something in common. She was as beautiful as she had been when he had worked with her years ago.

Lacy brought her grandfather the cinnamon roll, then he got out of his chair and hugged her. "I'm glad we can work this out between us."

"There is nothing to work out. You were right in the way you reacted when hunters killed Grandmother. I should have considered how devastated you were when it happened, and then I added to all the distress by not trusting that you had done what you had to do. You have Mrs. Fitz to thank for making me see the light."

He appreciated that she had helped with Lacy's turnabout regarding their disagreement. He ate his cinnamon roll and drank his coffee.

Lacy refilled his cup. "Do you want anything else?"

About then, some other customers arrived.

"No. I'm good. Thanks, Lacy."

"What are you going to do for the rest of the day?"

"Go shopping. I need something to wear to a Christmas dance."

She smiled. "I know. I was thinking the same. I didn't expect to be going to anything like that when I arrived here."

"You'll save me a dance?"

"I sure will." Then Lacy took orders from the customers at two other tables.

He drank the rest of his coffee, then left to check out of the motel. He needed to do it by ten, and then he would just keep his bags in his car and go shopping.

He was so glad Lacy had called him and let him know where she was and that she was safe. He respected Florence's training and knew she would keep his granddaughter safe. He was glad she had taken her under her wing.

Once he checked out of the motel, he found a shop that was carrying formal and informal wear for women and men. He was really impressed that cougars seemed to run everything here.

"What are you looking for? Can I help? I'm the owner, Iris Hawthorn."

"Frank Everest. I'm visiting my granddaughter, Lacy. I need something to wear to the Christmas dance. I have no idea what everyone wears to it. Is it formal? Casual?"

"Casual. Though some dress semi-formally. But everyone's there to visit, enjoy the Christmas spirit, and have fun. Now, for the New Year's party, that's formal."

"It must be nice to have so many cougars in town."

"I love it. I came here a short while ago and opened my shop, and found everyone so welcoming and kind. Deputy Sheriff Chase Buchanan and his lovely wife, Shannon, opened their home to me for Thanksgiving, though several other families also offered. They invited me first, so I accepted their offer. I've heard Lacy is here because of the trouble she had with an abusive ex-boyfriend."

"She is."

"Well, we have his picture, and if any of us see him, we will report him."

"That's great." He was amazed at how the cougars stuck together like that. He'd never lived any place like it.

He was considering moving here, particularly if Lacy was staying here. He wanted to be part of her life and enjoy seeing her as she married and had kids, so he could spoil them. She was all he had left in the world.

"Will you be taking Lacy to the dance?"

"Uhm, no, she's going with Rory."

"Oh, he's so cute, charming, a real nice guy."

"I'm going with Florence Fitzgerald. We worked together in the FBI years ago."

"Oh, my, how wonderful. Well, Mrs. Fitz wears wool skirts and sweaters, sometimes red or green sweater dresses for the dances, if that helps you to decide what to wear."

He was glad Iris could help him decide what to wear. He hadn't gone to anything like this since he'd lost his mate.

He ended up picking out a red wool sweater and dress pants. He decided to go whole hog and bought a pair of Western boots and a ten-gallon hat.

"Enjoy the dance."

"Are you going?" he asked.

"I'll be there. I might not have a date, but I'm going. From what I understand, others will dance with you, no matter your age, if you are alone. So I look forward to it."

"That sounds good." He paid for his clothes and then took them out to the car. Then he dropped by the sheriff's office to speak to law enforcement about Lacy's ex-boyfriend. "Hi, I'm Frank Everest. My granddaughter, Lacy, is working for Florence Fitzgerald. I've heard you are well aware of Lacy's ex-boyfriend."

"I'm Dan Steinacker, sheriff of Yuma Town." He shook Frank's hand.

"Chase Buchanan, part-time deputy sheriff and owner of the Pinyon Pines Resort on Lake Buchanan." Chase offered his hand in greeting, and Frank shook it.

"Stryker Hill, full-time deputy sheriff." Stryker shook his hand.

"I'm Ricky Jones, also a deputy sheriff."

"I'm a retired FBI agent. I worked with Florence Fitzgerald on cases and am moving in with Lacy and Florence for the time being."

"Hell, that's great news," Dan said, brightening.

"Yeah, we can always use another law enforcement officer in our community," Chase said.

"I agree. Florence has been instrumental in helping with cases in the past, despite being retired," Stryker said.

"I would be glad to help with any cases that come up." Being retired and having lost his mate, Frank had felt unsure about what to do with his life. This seemed like the perfect place to start over again.

Dan gave Frank the link that connected all the cougars so he could keep up with what was going on.

They all welcomed him to Yuma Town, and feeling really great that he was there, he headed over to the real estate office and walked into the brick building.

A woman immediately got up from her desk and said, "I'm Aya Noble. Are you looking for a rental or a home to buy?"

"Frank Everest." He was thinking of buying a home, but then he had the crazy thought that if he and Florence really hit it off, it might be better just to rent a place and give them time to get to know each other and see where it went. "A rental. Apartment or condo?"

"We have both of which are furnished. And they're available so you could move in right away."

Then he reconsidered. "Let me think on that." Frank was going to stay with Florence and Lacy first at Florence's home, and see where it went. Then, if nothing worked out between him and Florence, he would buy a house.

"Okay, sure. I'll be here if you ever need to buy or rent. Merry Christmas!"

"Merry Christmas." It was time for lunch, and he didn't want to overwhelm Lacy with constant visits to the coffee shop, so he decided to go to the pizza parlor. But then he thought he should ask Lacy if she wanted to join him.

Lacy answered her phone. "Yeah, Granddad?"

"I'm going to the Sizzling Slice for lunch. Do you want to join me?"

"I'm going there with Rory for dinner. Would you like to have lunch with Mrs. Fitz?"

"Uh, well, sure, if she wants to."

"Let me ask. Would you like to have lunch with my grandfather at the Sizzling Slice?" Lacy asked Florence. "Ava and I have this."

"Sure," Florence said.

"Are you going now?" Lacy asked her grandfather.

"Yeah, I'll come pick her up." He was old school and believed the guy should pick up the gal to take her to lunch, but he knew Florence was headstrong and might prefer to drive herself.

"Okay, I'll let her know."

They ended the call, and he headed over to the coffee shop. When he arrived, he expected Florence to be working on some of her cakes or pastries, but she was grabbing her coat, looking eager to eat lunch out. She smiled broadly at him.

He was glad she wanted to share a meal with him. It was much more fun to have company. She smelled sweet, of sugar, cinnamon, and nutmeg, and she was wearing a green sweater featuring a gingerbread girl and boy, holding red and green candy canes and a green wool skirt.

"Thanks for inviting me to lunch. Now that Lacy is helping Ava and me, I can take some me time, and they can too. It's working out great."

"That's wonderful. I'm glad to enjoy lunch with you."

They ended up ordering a pizza with red sauce, extra cheese, black olives, pepperoni, dried tomatoes, mushrooms, and bell peppers. Just the way he liked it, and he was glad she liked the same things as he did. They both asked for Italian lemonade.

"What made you come to Yuma Town?" he asked as they received their drinks.

Their pizza arrived, and they began eating slices.

"I was working a case. The woman had murdered her husband and fled before we could take her into custody. She told the police it was a case of suicide. By the time the autopsy came back a month later, proving it was murder, Willamina Caruso had fled the state. We split forces, and I ended up tracking her down to the outskirts of Yuma Town. I enlisted the local sheriff's department, and we soon had her in custody. Deputy Sheriff Stryker Hill took her in his patrol car, and I led the way back to Orlando, Florida.

"But once I had seen that cougars ran Yuma Town, I vowed to return there once I retired."

Frank nodded. "I've been thinking about Lacy, and if she truly has found a home here, I want to settle here too."

"It's a great place to be. You'll love it here."

"Yeah. She's all I have in this world, and I can't imagine living anywhere else. If she and Rory end up mating and have children, I want to be there for the great-grandchildren."

Florence smiled. "I can see you bouncing the kids on your knees."

"Yeah. I love kids."

"Me too. We'll have dinner at my house tonight. Do you want to go for a cougar run after that?"

"Yeah, I haven't done that in a long time," he said.

"You're all right with it?" She sounded worried, like she realized after losing his mate on a cougar run, he might be reluctant to do it.

"I would love to. It's in our nature to run as cougars. I haven't run with anyone in a good long while."

"I haven't either. We'll have a great time."

"We will."

Then they finished their pizza, and he drove her back to the shop. He expected to meet Rory having lunch with Lacy, but he wasn't. Since he was a ranch hand, he would have a lot of work to do, and he would have to live out in the country. Frank guessed he would meet Rory later when he picked up Lacy from Florence's house.

"Thanks for lunch." Florence gave Frank a peck on the cheek. But then she handed him her keys. "Go ahead and settle in. There's no sense in you having to try to figure out what to do with yourself until I arrive home."

He smiled. "Thanks." But he had every intention of taking a drive out to Hal's horse ranch and checking out Rory. He couldn't help but want to meet him one-on-one, to ensure he was good for her after this business with Timothy.

He drove to Florence's house and dropped off his bags in the guest room that wasn't occupied, then called Dan for directions to Hal's horse ranch.

Dan gave him the address and told him how to get out there, and Frank thanked him, then drove off. When he finally reached the ranch, he was impressed. Everything was covered in snow: a beautiful ranch house, another one about three acres away, a bunkhouse, several barns, all decorated with Christmas lights and Christmas wreaths. He thought how cheerful the place looked.

A man soon greeted him, his hand outstretched. "I'm Ted, the foreman at the ranch. And you are?"

"Frank, Lacy's grandfather. I learned she was dating Rory."

Ted smiled. "You want to meet him? He's a great guy. All the ranch hands are. Rory is taking care of the horses in the barn, if you want to meet him in there."

"Sure, thanks." Frank stalked off to the barn and entered it to find a dark-haired, young man brushing down one of the horses.

Rory glanced at him, smiled, and offered his hand to shake Frank's. He had a firm handshake and a welcoming approach.

"I'm Frank, Lacy's grandfather."

Rory laughed. He sounded perfectly amused. "She told me you were an awesome FBI agent."

"She has had a bad deal with her last boyfriend. I had to make sure she was all right. Then she told me she was seeing you, and I wanted to meet you."

"Well, I had a similar experience as she has had with her ex, so I totally understand how she's feeling. But the woman I was dating luckily took off, and I didn't have to deal with her anymore. I have every intention of keeping Lacy safe when I'm around her."

"That's what I wanted to hear. I have every intention of making sure of the same thing."

"Everyone in Yuma Town will."

"Yeah, I spoke to Dan at the sheriff's office, and he assured me of the same thing. I'm staying at Mrs. Fitzgerald's home for now. So when you pick up Lacy, I'll be there."

"She's a retired FBI agent also."

Frank smiled. "Yeah, we worked together on some cases."

"Oh, that's great."

"Well, I'll leave you to do your work. Just take care of Lacy for me."

"I sure will."

Then Frank left the barn, feeling good about Rory. He seemed like a decent guy. Then he returned to Florence's house and checked her fridge and freezer to see what he could make for them for dinner. He had better call Florence first, though, and make sure it was all right with her. He called the coffee shop, and Lacy answered.

"Hey, Lacy, can I speak to Florence?"

"Uh, sure." She said to Florence. "Granddad wants to talk to you."

"Hello?"

"Hey, I'm at the house, and I was planning to make us dinner. What would you like me to make?"

"You cook?"

He laughed. "Yeah. My mate hated cooking, and I was always trying new things. How about shrimp pasta? I'll run to the grocery store and pick up some shrimp and anything else we need."

"Yeah, sure. That sounds good."

"All right. You'll be home at...?"

"Six, or a few minutes after."

"Okay." He was glad he could do something for her when she was letting him stay at her house. He realized that though they had disagreed on how to handle cases they had worked on together, they otherwise seemed really compatible.

After checking whether Florence had any of the ingredients he needed, he headed to the grocery store. He picked up the shrimp, other items he had to have, and pork tenderloin for tomorrow's dinner.

He went home, unlocked the door, and carried all the grocery sacks into the house. Right away, he saw the Christmas tree was on its side, ornaments broken, lamps turned over, and garland on the mantle thrown onto the floor.

His heartbeat quickening, Frank dropped the sacks of food on the dining room table and retrieved his gun from the car. He realized he smelled Timothy's fresh scent in the house. The bastard had to have entered through the back way, or he would have smelled him at the front of the house when he first arrived.

He got on his phone to call the sheriff. "Hey, this is Frank Everest. I'm at Florence's house, and Timothy broke in."

"We're on our way."

Frank ended the call, went back inside, and began looking for Timothy to see if he was still there. He didn't find him downstairs, so he went up the stairs. No matter what, he wanted to stop this guy before he could hurt Lacy.

He followed Timothy's scent to Lacy's room, where her clothes were thrown all around the room. Frank heard the floor creak. Before he could turn, something hard struck him in the head, and he went down in a dead heap on the carpeted floor.

5

As soon as Dan called Florence to tell her that Timothy had been at her house, she left the shop with Lacy, leaving Ava to close it up.

An ambulance was dispatched while Chase, Dan, Ricky, and Hal took off outside to look for Timothy. Stryker stayed at the house to protect Frank, Lacy, and Florence, though she had her gun out and was ready to shoot Frank's attacker if he suddenly returned.

Lacy was holding Frank's hand and wiping away tears when the EMTs arrived and took him to the clinic, Lacy riding with him.

Stryker and Florence checked over the house again to ensure Timothy wasn't hiding somewhere inside. They discovered he had broken Lacy's bedroom window and used a trellis to climb up to it. Shattered glass was on the carpet. Stryker took photos.

Lacy's clothes were scattered all over the carpeted floor and bed. Furious, Florence didn't know what had been taken, if anything.

"Are you all right?" Stryker asked when they returned to the living room, and he took photos of her broken decorations and the toppled Christmas tree.

"Yeah. But I'm worried about Frank and Lacy."

"Why don't you go over to the clinic. I'll clean this up for you."

"All right." The mess in the living room wasn't important at all compared to Frank's well-being and Lacy's safety. "Will you be safe?"

"Yeah. I've got a couple of reserve officers coming to help me here. And Rory is on his way to the clinic to offer extra protection."

"Okay. I'm on my way then." The groceries were on the counter, so she put the items that needed refrigeration away before she left.

She was surprised that no one in town had seen Timothy before he arrived at her house. She assumed he had decided that, since the audio device had been destroyed when Lacy's trackers showed she was in Yuma Town, he had gone looking for her here first.

When Florence arrived at the clinic, she was directed to room four, where she found Dr. Kate, but Frank and Lacy weren't there.

"He's gone in for an MRI," Kate said. "He's conscious now. I need to see if he has any internal injury."

"Is he talking?"

"Yes. He didn't remember that he'd been struck at first, but the first thing he asked about was the groceries sitting on the dining room table."

"I put them in the fridge."

"He'll be glad to hear it."

Rory hurried into the room and frowned. "Where are Lacy and Frank?"

"Frank's getting an MRI. Lacy is with him."

Rory rubbed his lightly bearded chin. "Hell. How did he find Lacy?"

Florence explained what she thought had happened.

Then Frank was brought back to the room in a wheelchair, Lacy pushing it.

"I'm so sorry," Frank said to Florence.

"Nothing to be sorry about. I'm just glad you're all right."

"I should have stopped him, not been a punching bag."

"You shouldn't have gone into the house when you smelled his scent." Lacy gave him a reproachful look as he climbed into the bed with Lacy's help.

Kate was looking at the MRI scan on her computer. "Looks good. I'm keeping you under observation overnight. If you feel dizzy, nauseous, have blurred vision, or anything else that is unusual, let me know."

"Thanks, Doc. But I really am fine."

"Ah-uh."

Frank looked at Lacy and Rory. "Go. Have dinner tonight, you can drop by here later to check on me."

"Do you want me to pick up something from the Taco Shop?" Florence asked. "Or we could have it delivered."

"Sure, that would be good. Did you find the groceries on the dining room table?"

"I did. I put them in the fridge. If you go home tomorrow and feel better, I can help you make the dinner you had planned for us. We may have to skip the cougar run. We'll see what Dr. Kate says."

"Are you sure you'll be all right?" Lacy asked her grandfather.

"Yeah. Florence is staying with me and we'll have dinner together. You two run along."

Just then, Leyton Hill showed up. He was a Cougar Special Forces agent. "I'll be here for your protection." He saw the gun on the bedside table. "Though it looks like Mrs. Fitz might have things in hand."

"Better than I have." Frank sounded annoyed with himself.

"We've all had someone get the best of us in this line of business at one time or another," Leyton said. "I'm Leyton Hill, by the way, special agent with the Cougar Special Forces. Dr. Kate is my mate."

"He was wounded when he came into town and took Kate hostage. He took her on an unscheduled camping trip, initially," Florence explained. "Everyone was searching for her and her kidnapper."

"And she mated you?" Frank asked Leyton incredulously.

"Yeah, she's a very forgiving person." Leyton was all smiles.

Frank chuckled.

Florence figured Frank would get a kick out of it. He needed some cheering up. Then she pulled up the Taco Shop menu on her phone. "What would you like?"

Frank glanced over the menu. "The cheese enchiladas."

"Hmm, I'm going to get the cheese and spinach enchiladas. Anything to drink?"

"Lemonade."

"Me too." Then she ordered it and told them where to deliver it, deciding that was the best option while she stayed with him. "They said it would take about half an hour."

"Okay."

Florence pulled up a chair. "Did you see Timothy?"

"No. I just smelled his scent in the air. I heard the floor creak, but before I could turn and confront him, he struck me, and I guess I was out for the count."

"You sure were."

"I'm glad neither you nor Lacy had been there at the time. No telling what he would have done."

"I wish I had been there for you. You didn't call for backup?"

"I did."

"But you didn't wait for them."

"I wanted to make sure he didn't get away."

"We need to stop him for sure, but your life and safety are more important."

Shannon called Florence, and she answered the phone.

"Hey, Stryker and Chase are at your home, cleaning up the mess the housebreaker made. Tracey and I are dropping by, and we're going to help them clean up."

"Oh, thanks so much. I'm staying at the clinic until Frank's ready to sleep for the night."

"Leyton, Chet, and Dan are also going to take turns watching over you. Hal wants Lacy to stay at his and Tracey's home until we catch this guy," Shannon said. "He's calling her about it, but they have three ranch hands and Ted and Hal to watch over her there, since Timothy is after her. We all believe Frank was collateral damage."

"That sounds good."

"You and Frank will still be safeguarded at home or the clinic until this guy is caught."

"All right. I think I'm going to need a bunch of security cameras. I never needed them before." Florence was glad they would be watching over them.

"We'll make sure it's done."

"Thanks." After they ended the call, Florence called Ava to make sure she was all right.

"Yeah, Nina came to safeguard the shop as soon as Frank was hurt. She even helped me serve customers until closing."

"Oh, wonderful." As a deputy sheriff, Nina was perfect for the job.

"I'm fixing dinner. Will you be at the coffee shop tomorrow?" Ava asked.

"Yes. Someone will be watching Frank whether he's home or at the clinic."

"Nina said she would be at the shop all day tomorrow in case Timothy realizes Lacy works there."

"She'll be at the ranch. I don't want her working until they catch this guy."

"I understand. I'll check with you later," Ava said.

"See you tomorrow." Then they ended the call.

Not long after that, Frank and Florence's enchiladas and drinks were delivered, and they enjoyed each other's company as they ate.

Dan called her then. "Hey, I just wanted you to know that we found the perp's car and have confiscated it. He won't be going very far without it. Also, we have your guest room window repaired, and I want to ask you if you want us to remove the trellis."

"Yeah, sure. We don't want him to come in that way again."

"Okay. We'll take it down and place it in the garden for now. Hopefully, you can use it in the garden as an architectural feature when the snow has melted in the spring."

"I like that idea. Thanks."

Then they ended the call, and she finished her meal. Frank ate the last of his enchiladas. She was glad he had a good appetite, but he appeared worn out.

"I'm going to let you get some rest." She wanted to go home and straighten the mess up at home so that when she took Frank there, he wouldn't have to see how awful it was again.

"You be safe." He reached out and squeezed her hand.

She kissed him on the cheek. "I will be. You too. And I'll be in to see you tomorrow before I go to the shop."

"All right."

Then she left him for the night and said goodnight to Leyton, who was sitting outside the room.

"Night. Do you need someone to follow you home?" Leyton asked.

"No. I'll be home before you know it, and Stryker or someone else will be there to watch over me."

"Okay. Call him to let him know you're on your way home."

"All right, I will." She got into her car and called Stryker on the way home. "Hey, it's Florence. Are you still at my house?"

"Yeah."

"I'm on my way home."

"All right. See you in a few."

She soon pulled into the garage and closed the garage door. Stryker opened the door for her. "How's Frank doing?"

"He's okay. Hopefully, he won't have any complications tonight."

"I sure hope not."

She looked at the tree and couldn't believe it. "Oh, my."

"Shannon and Tracey brought ornaments over and replaced your broken ones. The Christmas lights were fine."

"It looks beautiful."

"They did a nice job on it. Every time I tried to put balls up, they kept telling me that I needed to space them out and watch that I didn't add too many of the same color in the same place. My dear mate always decorates our tree with the kiddos."

Florence laughed. She could envision it. She would have to call them and thank them later. It was late, and she needed to see Frank early before she went to the coffee shop. "I'm off to bed. If you need anything or hear anything, let me know."

"I sure will."

She headed upstairs to take a shower but peeked into Lacy's room first. Her clothes were gone. She guessed she had come by and packed them up and then went to Hal's ranch. The window had been replaced, and the broken glass had been cleaned up.

Florence sighed. She was so glad that everything had been straightened up. And she was relieved that Lacy was staying at the ranch with all the protection she would have there.

Once Florence was in her polar bear pajamas, slippers, and a robe, she went downstairs to make some cocoa before bed. "Would you like cocoa topped with whipped cream?"

"Yeah, that would be great," Stryker said.

"You can sleep on the couch. I'll bring you some bedding, and you can watch things down here. I'll take care of the second floor."

"Sounds good to me."

"If you're hungry or thirsty, just feel free to eat and drink whatever you would like."

"Thanks."

Then they drank their cocoa, and she put the penguin mugs into the dishwasher. She brought out sheets, a red-and-green plaid blanket, and a pillow, and he helped her make a bed on the couch.

"Thanks, Florence."

"Thank *you* for everything. I kept envisioning coming home to a Christmas catastrophe, but I am so thankful that you had cleaned up the mess and the ladies decorated everything." Then she said goodnight, but on the way up to the room, her phone rang, and she saw it was the clinic. She worried Frank had taken a turn for the worse. But it was Frank calling.

"Hey, is everything all right there?" he asked.

"Oh, yes. Everything was cleaned up, and a couple of ladies redecorated the Christmas tree. Lacy's window was replaced." Florence let out her breath. "I miss you." She really did. She had been alone for so long that she hadn't realized how much she missed having a remarkable man in her life.

He chuckled. "I missed you as soon as you left. Lacy and Rory came by. They said they had picked up her clothes while you and I were eating dinner here, and then they had driven out to the ranch."

"Do you want me to stay there with you tonight?"

"Nah. I'm going to sleep, and the couch here won't be that comfortable. Hopefully I'll be with you tomorrow."

"I sure hope so. Get a good sleep, Frank. I'm off to bed myself."

"Sweet dreams."

"Hope yours are too." Though she worried he would have nightmares about being struck on the head and knocked out. But she truly looked forward to seeing him tomorrow.

Then she got a call from Lacy, which she wasn't expecting. "Are you sure you don't want me to come into work tomorrow?"

"I think you would be safer at the ranch. He probably doesn't know you are staying there, but he could know that you're working at the coffee shop."

"Okay."

"Did you have fun with Rory tonight?"

"I did, but I felt a dark cloud was hanging over me because of

Granddad getting hurt and knowing that Timothy is in the area. But I also worry about you. He knew I was staying at your house. What if he returns there, looking for me? Or takes you hostage to get to me?"

"Someone will be with me. I'm sure that someone will be at the shop with us tomorrow also."

"All right. Well, if you need me to help, let me know."

"I will, thanks, Lacy." But Florence really wanted Lacy to stay out at the ranch. She felt Lacy would be safer there, and she suspected Hal would stay as a deputy sheriff to protect her, just in case her ex learned where she was.

Rory felt terrible about Lacy's grandfather, and if he ever caught sight of the cougar who did it, he would kill him. Cougars like that didn't go to prison. They were a security risk if they were incarcerated because they could change into their cougar at any given time.

He knew Lacy had been having difficulty concentrating on eating her dinner at the Sizzling Slice. She'd called Mrs. Fitz to make sure she was all right.

"Do you want to go to bed?" Rory asked Lacy, rubbing her arms with tenderness in the entryway to Hal and Tracey's home.

"I still want to go for a cougar run, if you want to do it."

"Yeah, sure." He was thrilled, but he figured she wanted to do it to work out some pent-up frustration over what had happened to her grandfather and the concern that her ex now knew she was in Yuma Town. "You...aren't planning on running again, are you?"

He considered she might want to because of her past actions when her ex caught up to her.

"No." She wrapped her arms around Rory, hugged him, and kissed him on the mouth, lightly at first, and then the kiss morphed into a promise to stay with him.

He embraced her tightly, telling her he was there for her and she didn't have to worry about Timothy any longer.

"I have you and all of Yuma Town to back me up this time." She smiled. "And I think Granddad and Mrs. Fitz are hitting it off. I wouldn't want to ruin that for them by leaving, knowing my grandfather would just come after me again to try and keep me safe."

"Good. I think so, too, about your grandfather and Mrs. Fitz. I haven't seen her that giddy since she sat on Santa's lap at the women's tea last Christmas. I have a special place I'll take you to then."

She laughed about Mrs. Fitz sitting on Santa's lap. "I'm looking forward to seeing your special place." She led him to her guest room, and they both removed their clothes and shifted into cougars, then raced down the stairs as Tracey and Hal were getting their kids ready for bed. All four of them: Tabitha, Denise, Liam, Evan Chase were eight years old, but turning nine on December 29th. They always had a big party for the quadruplets.

The kids made Rory think of having children with Lacy. He smiled, and they headed out the cougar door and into the cold, snow-covered ground. The full moon shone in all its glory as they ran across the snow-covered fields, its light reflecting on the snow. He was taking her to everyone's favorite spot. A waterfall now frozen in an icy sculpture that was just beautiful.

When they reached the river, it was flowing, though the banks were covered in ice. She just stared at the waterfall in all its frozen glory. She licked Rory's nose, telling him he had done right by bringing her here.

He licked her back and nuzzled her muzzle. She reciprocated, then headed closer to the waterfall. Icy rocks were right next to the riverbank like steppingstones to the waterfall.

He knew she was going to navigate the rocks before she even moved in that direction. He wanted to warn her that they were slippery, but she could see that they were.

Then she gingerly climbed onto the first of the boulders. He was right behind her. Not that he could stop her from falling into the river if she slipped off the rocks. Then she went to the next rock, and he waited for her to reach the next boulder. Once she was on it, he moved to the rock behind her and promptly slipped off the rock into the water.

He wanted to laugh. She leapt into the water after him, but he was okay. He appreciated that she worried about him though. He climbed back up on the rocks, and she joined him. Then she continued to the waterfall and licked the ice sculpture. She was cute.

She managed to work her way behind the frozen waterfall, and he joined her. She licked his wet fur, and he licked hers. He'd been behind the waterfall before, but not when it was frozen! It was like looking through a distorted version of the world.

Thankfully, their cougar coats were keeping them warm. They cuddled together, and he enjoyed the warmth they shared.

Then Lacy rubbed against Rory and began to leave the cave behind the waterfall and quickly stopped. Rory ran into her, but looked around her to see what the matter was. A cougar he didn't recognize was standing on the boulders, teeth bared.

Aww, shit. If they were wolves, they could howl for backup. But as cats, their screeches couldn't carry as far as a wolf's howl. He moved past her and tore into the cougar. He smelled his scent then and knew it was the ex.

He was a little heavier than Rory, but Rory was more muscled. And damned determined to kill the cougar before he harmed Lacy.

But she was just as angry with the cougar as Rory, and she began tearing into him like Rory was. They'd all fallen in the water and were struggling to keep their heads above it while fighting him.

Timothy finally made it to shore and tore off. He might think he could bully his ex-girlfriend, but he couldn't take on Rory and Lacy at the same time. They raced after him. He was headed for the ranch, but then he must have thought better of it because they could get reinforcements, and he took off for the Rocky Mountains.

Rory considered chasing after him, but both he and Lacy were bleeding, though so was Timothy. Lacy was trying to catch her breath. Rory nudged her to return to the ranch with him.

They headed back at a lope. He couldn't believe the bastard would figure out where Lacy had ended up, though he knew once Timothy had reached the ranch, he would have smelled their scents. He probably was irritated beyond measure that Lacy was running with Rory on a cougar date.

Once they reached the ranch, they headed straight for Hal and Tracey's home. Lacy led the way inside and ran up the stairs, startling Tracey.

"Ohmigod, what happened to..." Tracey began to say, then saw Rory right behind Lacy, bleeding also.

Tracey called out, "Hal, we have trouble."

EVEN THOUGH LACY and Rory had been torn up a bit by her ex, Timothy had suffered the brunt of the fight. She wished he would die in the mountains, but that probably wouldn't happen with their faster healing genetics.

Both Lacy and Rory put on their underclothes but needed to have their wounds cleaned and bandaged. They would heal in half the time that it took humans to heal, but they still had some pretty deep bite marks.

"I'm taking them to the clinic," Hal said, after looking at their bite marks. "Kate said she would be there when we arrive."

Lacy and Rory got dressed. "Thanks, Tracey," Lacy said.

"I'm so sorry this has happened," Rory said.

"I just wish we could have killed him." Lacy pulled on her sweater.

"Where did he go?" Hal asked. He paused his conversation on the phone.

"Up into the mountains," Rory said. "Since both of us were injured, I wanted to return Lacy home and get our wounds bandaged."

"You did the right thing," Tracey said.

"I wanted to go after him, believe me," Rory said.

"I did too." Lacy squeezed his hand.

Hal said on the phone. "Okay, Dan. We're going to the clinic. I'll let Ted know to alert our men to keep my family safe and to keep a watch out for this guy."

Then they left in Hal's pickup truck to get medical care. "Should we tell Mrs. Fitz?" Rory asked Lacy.

"No. We can tell her tomorrow. Though since Stryker is staying with her, he probably needs to be informed. We can check in on Granddad, but I don't want to wake him if he's sleeping."

"I agree."

When they arrived at the clinic, Dr. Kate looked over their injuries and stitched up three wounds on Rory's shoulder and back and two on Lacy's throat. She was lucky Timothy hadn't killed her.

Rory was sure if Timothy could have, he would have ended her life by the river. They had to eliminate him first.

6

———

Frank was dozing when he heard Lacy's voice as she talked to Rory while they headed down the hall past his room at the clinic. He had been sleeping on and off. Then he worried that Lacy had been hurt. Why would she be here otherwise, if not to see him? He didn't think she would be at the clinic so late.

He pushed the nurse's call button, and she responded. "Yes, Mr. Everest?"

"Is Lacy here?" Maybe he had thought he had heard her voice, but really hadn't in his fog-filled mind.

"Oh, yes. Her ex-boyfriend fought Lacy and Rory as cougars on a run. Dr. Kate came in to take care of their bite and claw marks."

"Aww, hell. I suppose Timothy is still running free."

"Yeah, but Rory said he was chewed up worse than they were and headed for the mountains."

"Can I see them?"

"I'll let them know you're awake and you want to see them. But Dr. Kate needs to take care of them first."

"Of course." Frank was so angry that Timothy had hurt Lacy and Rory, he wanted to get out of bed and find the bastard and finish him himself. He was wide awake when Lacy and Rory came in to see him. "What happened?"

Lacy explained their cougar run, Timothy tracking them as a cougar, and the fight. "Dan called us and said they're initiating a cougar hunt before dawn. I want to go with them, but he said no."

"I did too, but Dan wants me to stay with Lacy, which I certainly agree with," Rory said.

"How bad are your injuries?" Frank asked.

"Some stitches for bites and wicked claw marks," Lacy said, "but you know how it is with our healing genetics. They'll all be healed up before long. Not Timothy's wounds, since he isn't getting any treatment for them. His injuries will take longer to heal."

Frank scoffed. "He should be dead." He was thinking about the beauty of the holidays, and that things between him and Lacy had improved by a hundred percent. As far as meeting up with Florence and Lacy having Rory in her life, he couldn't be more thrilled. But this business with Timothy needed to end.

"Yeah, we agree," Rory said. "I'm staying with Lacy, but others will be trying to track him down in the meantime."

"I'm glad both of you are all right," Frank said, realizing he should have said that to begin with.

"We've all had a time with Timothy today," Lacy said.

"Yeah, I agree." Frank just hoped Florence would remain safe.

Lacy gave Frank a light hug. "We're going to the ranch and return to bed. We're exhausted after all that has happened."

"Stay safe, honey." Frank hugged her back and shook Rory's hand.

"I'll keep her safe." Rory took her hand and led her out of the room.

Frank knew Rory would if he could. He didn't blame them for running as cougars on the ranch, not expecting Timothy to attack them. The guy just had a knack for finding Lacy, even without tracking devices to guide him. Now he would know Lacy was seeing another guy, and Frank knew Timothy would be even more infuriated and intent on getting her back. He was definitely a loose cannon.

Frank was soon asleep, and it seemed as though he had hardly slept when he felt a light kiss on his cheek and a hand on his. Then he smelled her light floral scent. *Florence.* He smiled.

"I'm heading to the shop. We go in early to start baking. I didn't want to wake you, but I wanted to see you before I went to work."

"I'm glad that you did."

"Can I bring you something special from the shop?"

"A raspberry scone and coffee?"

"Yeah, sure. I'll be back with it as soon as I can."

"No rush. I know Lacy's no longer helping at the shop for now. and you'll be busy serving customers."

"We'll have it covered."

Then she kissed his forehead and hurried off.

Now that was a nice way to wake up in the morning. Then Dr. Kate arrived to see him. "Well, good news. You can go home now, but if you feel like you want to stay here longer, until Florence closes shop and can go home with you, you can."

"No, I'm fine. I feel great. I would love to be home."

"All right. I'll give the orders to release you." Dr. Kate left the room.

Frank called Florence then to give her a heads-up. "Hey, Dr. Kate released me from the clinic. I'll have Stryker bring me to the shop for breakfast, and he can have some too. And then he can drop me off at the house."

"Okay, that works. Ask him what he wants, and we'll make that up for him," Florence said.

Frank got out of bed and went to the door. "Hey, Stryker, I'm being released."

Stryker smiled. "Good show. Do you want to get dressed, and I'll take you home?"

"Yes, but first we're making a stop at the coffee shop. Florence is making me breakfast. What would you like? It's on me."

"French toast and coffee would be good."

"Did you hear?" Frank asked Florence.

"Yep, getting it ready right away."

"Okay, we'll be over there in a few." Frank closed his door and got dressed. He was glad he wasn't feeling dizzy or otherwise incapacitated. His former mate had always said he had a hard head.

FLORENCE WAS SO glad to see Frank up and about and eager to eat breakfast. She hugged him as he walked in the door to her coffee shop with Stryker, and Frank hugged her back and kissed her on the lips. "I enjoyed the morning wake-up."

She smiled. "I have both your breakfasts ready."

"Thanks," both Frank and Stryker said as they took a seat at one of the tables.

Some others were already there having breakfast and coffee. They weren't cougars, so Florence figured they must be traveling through Yuma Town early in the morning.

Light snow was falling outside, the lights outside and in, reflecting off the white snow. Everything seemed quiet outside when it was snowing. Inside, the other family was eating quietly, except for the tinkling of a spoon stirring the sugar into a cup of coffee. They looked like they were half asleep. The little boy who looked like he was about four, had his elbow on the table and his hand propping up his chin, his eyes shuttering closed.

The girl was eating a muffin so slowly that Florence didn't think they would ever finish breakfast at this rate.

She brought out Frank's and Stryker's orders, and Ava served up their coffee, cream, and sugar.

"Thanks," the guys said.

Then they began adding sugar and cream to their coffee and eating their pastries.

Some more customers arrived, and Florence went to wait on them. Frank called Lacy, hoping it wasn't too early, and told her he was going home.

"Granddad, are you okay?"

"Yeah, I just wanted you to know Dr. Kate released me so I'm going home after I have breakfast at the coffee shop."

"How are you feeling?"

"Great. How about you?"

"A little sore where I had some of the deeper bites, but otherwise, I'm fine," Lacy said. "The same with Rory. Ted gave him off the day from ranch work, and he's supposed to be my shadow."

"I'm glad to hear that."

"You're going to be protected at all times?"

"Yeah."

"I'm going to a sexy Santa's tea tonight. It was supposed to be in the afternoon, but too many Christmas events going on. Mrs. Fitz was planning to go, but she might not so she can stay with you. Though it's a female-only event, except for the sexy Santa, Rory is going to be there for my protection. I thought maybe you could also, so that Mrs. Fitz can still have fun at the event."

Frank chuckled. "Sure. I'll let Florence know I'm going to be there too for her." He was looking forward to seeing Florence and Lacy enjoy themselves and watching over the women with Rory.

"Tomorrow is the dance. You and Mrs. Fitz are still going, right?" Lacy asked.

"Yeah, for sure."

"Good. So Rory and I will be there too."

"That's great. Save me a dance."

"I sure will, Granddad."

They ended the call and he finished his breakfast.

"You're going to the dance with Mrs. Fitz on Saturday?" Stryker asked.

"Yeah."

"Good. A bunch of us will be there dancing with our mates while the kids have a holiday party. That way we'll still be watching over you and Lacy," Stryker said.

That made Frank want to go even more, if he'd had any thought of just staying home.

"Rory and I will be at the Sexy Santa event tonight so no one has to guard us."

"Oh, one of us will be there, taking his mate to the event, and will safeguard you and Lacy. Mrs. Fitz too, because we don't trust that Timothy might not come after her and take her hostage since Lacy works for her now."

"That sounds good."

They left their table, and Frank went to say goodbye to Florence. "Hey, I heard about your Sexy Santa tea party. I'll be there."

She laughed, wrapped her arms around his neck, and kissed his mouth. He embraced her soundly and kissed her back. "You just want to make sure I don't fall for the sexy Santa."

He smiled. "Yeah, that's it. And we're still going to the dance together."

"For sure. You're not getting out of that. I hope you like to dance."

"I do."

"Good, then we'll have a great time. I'll see you at the house, and then we'll go to the tea party."

"Yeah. What should I wear?" he asked, though he wasn't really attending, just being there for her.

"Something Christmassy, red sweater or green sweater. Everything else is optional. Just no sexy Santa suit," Florence said.

He laughed out loud. "Trust me, I wouldn't."

Then they kissed, and he felt like things were going just the way they should as far as his relationship with Florence.

Then Frank said goodbye, and he and Stryker returned to Florence's home. They searched the whole house to make sure Timothy hadn't returned to it, but it was clear.

"I'm going to take a nap." Frank had been up so late and then woken early this morning, and was feeling sleepy.

"Are you okay?" Stryker asked.

"Yeah, just with seeing Lacy so late last night when she was injured and then Florence waking me so early and the nurses checking on me throughout the night, I'm tired."

"Okay, well, you get a good rest, and if you start feeling bad at all, just let me know, and I'll run you over to the clinic."

"Thanks." But Frank wasn't feeling bad, just tired. He was glad to see the Christmas tree standing and all the broken ornaments cleaned up and the tree decorated beautifully again. He glanced at Lacy's room. Her clothes that had been scattered all over the room were gone, and the window had been replaced. He was relieved she was staying at the ranch.

THAT NIGHT, Florence came home to the dinner that Frank had promised her before Timothy had knocked him out. "Everything smells so good."

"Chase is eating with us and taking us to the party. Shannon will meet us all there," Frank said, dressed in a red sweater, making him look nice and Christmassy, "even though Shannon told him that his being there could crimp her style."

Florence laughed.

Chase came inside to eat with them after doing a perimeter check. "No sign of anyone coming around the house. I would have smelled Timothy or seen footprints or paw prints in the snow. Dinner smells great."

"I'm glad you can enjoy it with us," Frank said, and served up the food while Florence got everyone water.

They all took their seats, enjoyed dinner, and then Florence dressed in a red dress, boots, and a white faux fur coat, Frank helping her into it before he put on his coat. "You look stunning," he told Florence.

"I love your red sweater, just perfect for the tea party," she said.

Then he took her hand and led her out to Chase's patrol car. Chase drove them to the community center, where the whole place was decorated with a Christmas tree, silver garland, red bows, and red-and-white candy canes. Treats of all kinds were sitting on a table, from cinnamon rolls to chocolate fudge.

Even though Frank wasn't really a guest since it was a women's tea party, Florence made him a Christmas plate of treats that he loved—chocolate fudge, maple fudge, and Pfeffernüsse cookies.

Now she knew what he really liked to have and she would make some for Christmas.

Lacy did the same thing for Rory, and he kissed her before he sat down on one side of the room with Chase and Frank.

Shannon hurried over with peppermint ice cream for Chase. He gave her a big hug and kiss. "You weren't supposed to be here, but I'm glad that you are," she told him. "But I'm still going to have fun."

"I want you to. Just ignore me."

Then all the women there whooped and hollered, and Florence said, "Got to go."

"Enjoy yourself," Frank said.

She would. Sexy Santa was Wyatt, one of Hal's ranch hands. He smiled at Lacy, but Florence was sure she was already taken. Despite having had a bad relationship with Timothy, Lacy appeared to have fallen in love with Rory at first sight, and he seemed to feel the same way about her. Florence was so glad for both of them.

Mistletoe hanging over his head, Wyatt sat down on the red velvet Santa throne wearing a Santa suit, no fake white beard, just wearing his own trimmed brown beard. Christmas music was playing overhead, "Jingle Bells" right this moment, and he patted his lap, inviting the ladies to sit there and have their photos taken.

Florence took hold of Lacy's hand and headed over to Wyatt, who was sitting on his throne, waiting for the ladies to get the courage to pose with him for pictures. They stood on either side of him, then took hold of his Santa jacket and opened it up even further to show off his abs, while clutching at the white fur trim. Then they leaned over to kiss each of his cheeks, while they posed with one leg up like they were a couple of chorus girls, excited about kissing Santa.

Laughter filled the room. Florence was glad that she and Lacy went first to show the other ladies they didn't have to just sit on Santa's lap for photos.

Then she and Lacy picked up some treats and went to sit by Frank and Rory. Normally, the guys wouldn't have been here, but they wanted to sit with them while they watched the other women sit on Santa's lap, or kiss his cheek as they had done.

Frank kissed Florence. "I don't think I've ever laughed as much as I have tonight. You ladies were adorable."

Florence chuckled. "It's a fun party, and we all give money to a special cause. Often, it's to add books to the library."

Rory pulled Lacy onto his lap and hugged her tight, as if he was afraid Wyatt might change her mind about who she wanted to be with. But she kissed his mouth, not his cheek, showing he was the one she had chosen for her own.

"I thought the same as you, Frank. The ladies were sweet. I wasn't sure what to expect. Especially of Wyatt," Rory said.

They all laughed.

Then Shannon finally sat on Wyatt's lap, crossed her legs at the ankle, straightened her legs out, leaned back, and laughed for her picture. Then she joined Chase.

"That was cute, Shannon," Chase said, kissing her.

She smiled and hugged him. "I didn't want to be too risqué as a married woman with twin girls."

Chase laughed. "Only Rory has to worry about Wyatt with Lacy, since none of them are mated."

"Nah," Lacy said. "Rory doesn't have to worry about that. It was all done in charitable fun."

"I have to admit that Wyatt can be charming when he wants to. And with a single cougar in our midst, he would certainly be interested in getting to know Lacy better." Rory took another bite of his cheesecake, covered in red and green M&Ms and sprinkles baked inside.

That was one of the Christmas treats Florence had donated to the tea party. Also the chocolate fudge and maple fudge decorated with icing snowmen and Christmas trees that Ava had created.

Everything was great, the music, the treats, the camaraderie, and the Christmas Santa, who was cute as he played his role perfectly for the part.

"You didn't want to be the Christmas Santa this year?" Florence asked Rory.

Rory shook his head. "Most of the bachelor males drew straws; the one with the longest straw was the winner. But I hadn't participated."

"Why not?" Lacy asked.

"I thought all the women attending would be mated. I could see getting a black eye from an angry husband."

Everyone laughed.

"We haven't ever had a mate become angry over his wife sitting on Sexy Santa's lap," Shannon said, smiling.

They finished their treats and began cleaning up the community center. The guys all helped, which was a welcome addition to the party this year. Once they were done, Chase would go home with Shannon. Travis MacKay, a CSF special agent, like Leyton, arrived to watch over Florence and Frank at their home next, while Rory would take Lacy back to the ranch. Hal's wife, Tracey, and Ted's wife, Stella, went with Lacy and Rory. Everyone said good-night and would be at the dance tomorrow night.

When Florence and Frank arrived home, Florence made cocoa for everyone, and they picked out a Christmas movie, *Jingle All the Way*, to watch.

Florence and Frank hadn't watched the movie in several years and were cuddling with each other and laughing at the Christmas comedy. Travis said, "My mate, Bridget, and our twin boys watched it last Christmas, one of our favorites."

"That was cute," Florence said as the movie ended. "I hadn't remembered how much fun it was." She began making up the bed on the couch for Travis while Frank put their cocoa mugs in the dishwasher.

They said goodnight to Travis, thanking him for watching over them, and then headed up the stairs.

"Do you want to join me in the master bedroom?" Florence asked Frank.

Frank smiled. "Are you sure?"

"Yep. In the holiday spirit and beyond, I am."

"Hell, yeah."

She figured that at their age, they didn't need to delay enjoying their golden years.

"I'll join you in just a minute." He headed for his guest room.

Even though Florence wanted this, she was afraid it would backfire. That she wouldn't like being with someone in bed after having not shared a bed in so long with her mate, that they might not be compatible, but they wouldn't know that for sure unless they tried it.

7

Frank didn't know what to do when he changed into his green pajamas, and Florence was already under the covers in reindeer pajamas.

He joined her in bed, not sure if she wanted to cuddle or sleep apart, but he moved in to kiss her, and they were sliding their hands over each other's bodies underneath their PJ shirts. He felt like a young man all over again. He loved this with her.

She was kissing his mouth and seemed to be just as wrapped up in the moment with him. When she went to loosen his pants, he was more than surprised, but perfectly willing to go further.

She began stroking him, and he was easily becoming aroused. He ran his hand over her full breasts, loving their softness and fullness, his thumb brushing against her firm nipples.

Adrenaline surged in them, setting every surface of skin humming with urgency, their breathing gone ragged and feral, as if they'd both been running for miles in the dark as cougars on a mission. Even the air between them seemed to thicken with the tang of sweat and musk, with the primal, almost animal perfume of their desire—her hands clutching at his back, his fingers working frantically at the drawstring of her pajama bottoms.

He groaned when he finally released the bottoms, when the bare skin of her hip came free, and the heat beneath her clothing smacked him like a fever. He was shaking, not with nerves but with a wild, unfamiliar need, his body overtaken by a single imperative. She continued to stroke him with firmness, just the right tightness sending him to the precipice.

His own climax came so fast it was almost an embarrassment, like a randy lad who couldn't last, but for once he didn't care, could only laugh hoarsely into the hollow of her throat as pleasure bucked through him.

Now it was his turn to pleasure her. He began to caress the area between her legs, drenched curly hairs, a swollen feminine nub eager for his touch. It took her more time to come, but he was patient and determined. She finally tensed so hard, he could sense her coming, her heart pounding frantically. She came with a spasmodic clenching of her channel, a low, almost bestial growl in her chest as her whole body seized and then went boneless.

"Ohmigod," was all she said, breathing hard, staring up at the ceiling with wide, incredulous blue eyes.

He lay beside her, lightheaded and spent, his forehead sticky with sweat, and for a long moment neither of them spoke, the only sound the ragged catch of their breathing and the blowing wind outside the windows on this wintry night.

He chuckled, running his hand over her tummy in a loving caress. "Shower?"

"Yeah, let's do it." She climbed off the bed, and he hurried to join her, tossing aside his pajamas on the way to the bathroom.

Once they were in the large master bathroom, he unbuttoned her pajama top and tossed it back into the bedroom to keep it from getting wet. Then he removed her pants and dropped them on her top while she started the hot water and climbed into the shower.

The sight of her lathering body wash across her chest left him breathless. When he reached for the soap and began tracing circles on her skin, she met his eyes with a smile that made his pulse quicken. Without a word, she took the bottle, squeezed a pearl of soap into her palm, and returned his touch with gentle, deliberate strokes of her own.

He never thought he would mate again after he lost his mate, but Florence had rekindled that love all over again. He was glad she had worked with him at the FBI, which gave them common ground. He was excited to spend the rest of his life with her.

They finished their shower and dried off. He didn't know if she would feel more comfortable with putting her pajamas back on, but when she climbed into bed naked, he did too. And then he wrapped his arm around her waist and kissed her cheek.

He thought of declaring his love for her at the dance, but he could be rather impulsive, just like she could be. He ran his hand through her hair, loving the softness. "I want to commit to you."

"Oh?" she asked, her blue eyes wide with interest.

"Yeah. There's no time like the present, as they say. I love you."

She laughed. "I thought the same thing. I love you too, and I invited you to my bed because I didn't want to wait."

He snuggled with her. "I'm so glad. Do you mind this? Or do you need your space?"

"I love this. The snow is falling outside. It's nearly Christmas. It couldn't be more perfect."

"My thought also."

Then they closed their eyes, and he thought he was the luckiest man in the world. They just needed to take Timothy out so their lives could return to normal, and they wouldn't have to have a police escort all the time.

In the middle of the night, she began caressing his back. Yeah, he was ready to mate her. Though from what he had learned about wolves, it wasn't the same. With them, after consummating a relationship, they were mated for life. Cougars, like other cats, didn't have that mindset. But the human part of them tempered their wild cat instincts, and for shifters, they could divorce, but they often didn't.

FLORENCE LOVED that Frank was proposing to her in a cougar's way and knew they would be happy together. He climbed on top of her, and she felt terrific, safe, and comforted. Then he entered her tight sheath, and she loved it, loved making love to him when she didn't think she would ever do that again with a man she really cared about.

He thrust into her like a young man, their hearts pounding like crazy, their pheromones circling the wagons. He kept pumping into her, kissing her breasts as she rubbed his back. Everything he did made her feel like a million bucks. Then he was climaxing and groaning out loud. He rolled off her, and she cuddled up next to him.

"You are everything I knew you would be in bed," she said.

"I feel the same way about you." Then he wrapped his arm around her and kissed the top of her head.

"THEY'RE GOING to do it, you know," Rory told Lacy as she joined him in his room at the bunkhouse. It was time for them to be a couple, or else Sexy Santa Wyatt might think he still had a chance with her.

They had decided that it would be better to stay at the bunkhouse so Hal's and Tracey's kids didn't hear them. Though they still had the other ranch hands who would. But they were all adults.

"You mean my grandfather and Mrs. Fitz?"

"Yeah."

She smiled.

"The way they kept kissing, holding hands, and whispering to each other, I know it's going to happen sooner or later."

"Maybe after the Christmas dance?" Lacy asked, stripping out of her clothes.

Rory hurried to remove his, nearly falling when he pulled off his jeans. She laughed. But then, perfectly naked, they began kissing and running their hands over each other. He knew that the first time he'd seen her at the coffee shop, she was the one for him. That's why he'd taken charge of introductions, proving he was an alpha.

So were the other ranch hands, but they hadn't been as quick to make their interest known, which worked for him. He kissed her mouth in a deliberately slow and seductive way. She responded, kissing him back with as much conquest. He loved how affectionate she was and how much she was into him, like he was her.

He ran his hands through her long, silky hair, and then they fell on the bed. Thankfully, it was a double, not a twin bed, though they would have made do.

He figured they would tell her grandfather they had decided to mate when they saw him at the dance tomorrow, and hope he was all right with them doing it so soon after meeting.

Then they were on the bed, writhing in the throes of passion, breathing in each other's musky scent, and enjoying every minute of it. This was the first time they had been able to do it in the comfort of a warm bedroom.

"I love you and everything about you," Rory said, then kissed her breast.

"I never expected to fall in love with a handsome ranch hand who would come to my aid when I needed a man in my life the most."

"I just wish you hadn't had to deal with your ex."

"I agree."

Then they pressed against each other, body to body, rubbing, gyrating, kissing each other deeply. Then he moved his body off hers to pleasure her before he entered her, wanting her to feel as much joy in the union as he would.

He brushed his hand down her belly, smelling her intrigue, her need. She put her hand on his neck in an endearing way, kissing him, as he started to move his questing fingers through her curly hairs and found her clit. He began to stroke her, soliciting delightful moans from her.

Then he dipped a finger into her wetness and began to stroke again, pressing harder. She arched her back with delight, eyes closed, as if lost in her emotions. He smelled her happiness and intense pleasure. He kept stroking, kissing her, and then she cried out.

He caught her mouth to stifle her cry. He knew the guys couldn't help but hear them making love because of their cougar hearing, but he didn't want her to feel embarrassed.

"Ready?"

"Yeah, past ready," she murmured.

He began to press his advantage and pushed deep inside of her. Then he began to thrust. He kept thrusting, kissing her, loving her, knowing that this was the perfect time for two cougars in love.

He came and growled. She laughed and kissed him again. Then they just cuddled together, and she said, "I love you."

"I love you too."

She sighed. "I wish we could run as cougars."

"I know, I do too. But we would have to take a bunch of cougars with us to run."

"Yeah, I hate Timothy for ruining this for us."

"We can do it. Just not this late at night. Everyone needs to get up early to work."

"Except for me."

"You can fix meals since you make such great dishes. All of us ranch hands cook, take turns, but it would be nice to have some of your home-cooked meals when we come in after a hearty day of work."

"I would love to."

"Ted taught us all to cook. None of us had a clue, so we'll definitely step in and help or make meals too."

"It'll be fun."

Rory was wondering if Hal and Tracey would give them some land to build on. That's what they had done with Ted when he and Stella mated. But he was the foreman.

That would be the icing on the cake if Hal and Tracey did. Rory would need to be near the ranch in any event so he could get there early enough to work. Then again, Lacy would have more of a drive to get to Yuma Town.

They would have to talk about it.

She was cuddled against his chest as if she were ready to go to sleep. But he was still so wound up about mating Lacy that he couldn't sleep. He was so happy. A cougar run would have helped.

Then Lacy licked his chest, and he realized, though it was dark out because of the time they always got up and that it was wintertime, that it was time to rise.

"You sleep in," Rory said.

"No way. I'm fixing breakfast." She kissed Rory and then slipped away before he could hug her.

Then he was out of bed, naked, and hugged her, kissing, not wanting to let her go.

She chuckled. "Maybe you can come in and have lunch with the others, but then linger a little longer before you join them to work."

"I'm sure that we can do that."

"Good." She then made everyone light, golden crepes filled with zesty orange cream and tart cranberry sauce.

Rory made side dishes of bacon and hash browns.

The guys all started joining them in the kitchen, checking out the crepes. Wyatt shook his head. "You sure got a bargain with capturing the filly's attention." Wyatt put out the silverware and napkins.

"We all do. We're getting a gourmet breakfast." Blaze set out plates. He chuckled when he saw the old-world Santa napkins. "Napkins? We just grab paper towels."

"We have a lady in our midst," Wyatt said.

8

L acy was glad to fix some special dishes she knew how to prepare for the guys. She really felt she should be working and not just sitting around all day. Maybe she could help Tracey with the kids or something.

Once the guys had finished eating breakfast, they offered to do the dishes, but it was the least she could do. "See you at lunchtime."

Then she cleaned up the kitchen and headed over to the main house. She knocked on the door, and Tracey answered it. "Hey, I need a job since I can't go to the coffee shop to work. Can I help you with anything? Make breakfast maybe for you and the kids?"

"Oh, I would love that. Then I can do the laundry."

"What do they like to eat?" Lacy wasn't sure the kids would enjoy the crepes she made for the guys. Kids could be kind of picky.

"Fix them whatever you like. If they don't care for it, they can have cereal instead."

"Crepes with orange cream and cranberry sauce."

"I would love it. They love cranberry sauce, so sure, go for it."

"Bacon, ham, or sausages to go with them?"

"Ham would be good."

"Okay, coming right up." Lacy went into the spacious kitchen, which was much more spacious than the bunkhouse kitchen. She was glad to be cooking for the Havertons because they allowed her to stay at the ranch.

She made breakfast for the family as Hal entered the house. She'd made enough for him too, just in case he was eating with the family.

"Whoa, we've got a gourmet breakfast this morning," Hal said as she served the food.

Tracey joined them, folding up a kitchen towel. "Hmm, that smells delightful."

Hal said, "I'll go get the kids."

"Do you homeschool them?" Lacy asked Tracey.

"I do. Though they're off for the Christmas holidays. We'll start back after New Year's Day." Tracey put the towel away and then set the table.

The kids ran down the stairs like a herd of gazelles.

"What's that?" Liam asked, taking his seat.

"Orange and cranberry crepes," Lacy said.

"Yum." Liam took a bite of them while everyone took their seats.

"Orange juice?" Lacy asked.

"Yeah, sure, that would be great," Tracey said.

Lacy got them all glasses of orange juice, then began cleaning the pans.

"I can't believe you're having Lacy make us breakfast when it appears she has already eaten," Hal teased.

"How else would we get such a beautiful breakfast treat?" Tracey said, enjoying her crepes.

"Mommy can't make this," Liam said, finishing his ham.

"Oh, sure she can," Lacy said. "But I love to cook so it's a pleasure for me to do so. Have you found anything about Timothy's whereabouts, Hal?"

She figured they might have had a search party look for him this morning, but maybe it had been too early.

"Right after we finish eating, we're headed out on horseback and in cougar coats," Hal said.

"We want to go," Tabitha said.

Hal ruffled her hair. "No kids."

"I want to go," Lacy said

Hal took a deep breath and let it out. "All right."

"Thanks." She understood why he didn't want her to go, but she had to be there if they found him. "I'll go as a cougar. I have only been on a trail horse, and he tried to dump me in the creek we crossed."

Hal laughed.

"We'll teach you how to ride," Tabitha and Evan Chase both said at the same time.

Lacy smiled. She figured that since she was mated to Rory, she would learn a lot more about ranch life, including riding horses. That way, she could ride with Rory across the land. That would be fun.

"The guys are just feeding the cows and horses," Hal said, taking his and Tracey's plates into the kitchen.

The kids finished their breakfast and then carried their plates into the kitchen. Tracey joined them and began putting them in the dishwasher.

"I already told them that we would be going on a hunt for Timothy after that." Hal got another cup of coffee.

"Who will be riding horseback?" Lacy asked.

"Only two of us. The others need to run as cougars because once we get to the mountains or rocky cliffs, we'll need to climb, and cats can do the job. Not the horses. But if we find a body, we'll bring it back by horseback." Hal drank his coffee.

Lacy was ready for this.

"Are you going to be all right running with your injuries?" Hal asked. "You and Rory can stay here if you can't shift yet."

"I'm sure of it." She hadn't thought about that. Both were still bandaged. But she thought they would do all right. She was sure that Rory would want to be on the hunt, not left behind to watch over her.

After cleaning up in the kitchen, she and Hal put on their jackets, hats, and gloves and went outside.

"Not that I'm trying to rush anything, but if you and Rory decide to mate, you can build a house on the acreage. We have tons, enough for each of our ranch hands to mate and build a home and live here. We need them on hand, but I understand you're working in town, and the two of you might want to build a home closer to town."

"I don't mind commuting." She loved how close everyone was at the ranch. Special trips into town for events like the dance would be fine, since she and Rory would go together.

Rory met with them and asked Lacy, "Are we staying or going?"

She appreciated that he asked her and didn't just assume one thing or another. "I'm good for going. How are you feeling?"

He smiled as if he were thinking of all their wild lovemaking last night.

She chuckled and felt her face warm with embarrassment. "Hal said we could build a home on the ranch's acreage. I'm good with that if you are."

"Are you sure? That makes it a bit of a drive for you."

"Yeah, it's like having a family here, and then we can go in and visit Granddad and do activities in town just like everyone else does. I don't mind commuting to work."

"Did you tell Hal we already mated?"

She smiled. "No. He just said when we did."

Rory hugged her. "I guess the truth is out then."

"Yeah, I was going to wait for us to tell everyone at the same time."

"I blew that."

She kissed him.

"It was inevitable," Hal said, laughing. Then he gathered everyone around. "Okay, we're going to hunt down Timothy, if we can find him," Hal said. "I want two volunteers to ride horses. The rest of us will run as cougars, and if we find him, we take him down."

"Permanently?" Rory asked.

"Yeah. We can't have him attacking Lacy, Rory, her grandfather, or any of our people further. He won't realize we have such a force to track him down," Hal said. "I'll go as a cougar. The rest of you decide who will ride the horses."

"I'm running as a cougar," Lacy quickly said. "I need to learn how to ride a horse."

"I'll be a cougar and stay by your side."

"I'll ride a horse," Wyatt said.

"Me too," Blaze said.

Then police cars drove up. More reinforcements.

Stryker, Travis, Chase, Ricky, and Leyton got out of the vehicles. "We're ready to go on the hunt. Dan is staying with Frank, and Nina is at the coffee shop with Ava and Mrs. Fitz," Stryker said. "Chet and Addie are searching for Timothy around town."

Blaze and Wyatt took off to saddle up a couple of horses.

"We're all going as cougars," Hal said. "You can use the bunkhouse to shift in. I'll meet you out here." Then he headed for the main house.

Everyone else went into the bunkhouse. Rory and Lacy went into his room and removed their clothes. They were still bandaged, and they just shifted. The bandages would most likely fall off when they ran, as they wouldn't stick to their fur very well. But she felt okay.

Rory seemed all right, too.

Then they all took off and fanned out, covering more territory. But Rory stayed close to Lacy. She knew he wasn't letting her out of his sight, and she loved him for it. She always felt so much safer with him around.

It had snowed a lot last night, so there were no tracks but one, and it wasn't a cougar's. It confused her. It was definitely a black bear's.

He should have been hibernating. She hoped they didn't run into a grumpy bear and have to deal with it.

She glanced at Rory, and he licked her muzzle. She licked his back, and they continued on their way. She noticed all the guys were standing in a line, as if they were searching for a crime victim or a missing person.

No one seemed to see anything, and they continued covering the land until they reached the forest below the cliffs. Now it would be more challenging to see each other as they continued to search for any sign of the cat. She kept glancing at the trees, making sure Timothy wasn't sitting on any of the branches near them. She kept smelling for his scent but didn't catch any sign of it.

They finally reached the base of the cliffs, and she looked to her left and right. Everyone was there, all having moved together to begin to navigate the cliffs. But then she saw movement in a cave up above. She stared at it, thinking it wasn't Timothy, but it was too big, dark brown, and furry.

The bear.

Everyone had been climbing the cliffs as cougars, but she couldn't believe it. Didn't anyone else see the bear peering out of the cave?

He growled, showing off long, wicked teeth.

She hesitated to climb the cliffs. He was directly in the path she had to take. Rory nudged her to go with him in that direction. He had to be crazy!

When she wouldn't budge, he wouldn't leave her. Rory suddenly shifted in this freezing weather. "That's John Blue Bearsden, a friend, and black bear shifter."

She couldn't believe it. She had never met a bear shifter before. She started up the cliffs, and Rory shifted and went with her. They reached the cave, and Rory greeted the bear.

He placed his massive paw on Rory's back and gently ran his paw over it. Then he nuzzled Lacy's face. She hadn't expected that, but now she knew his scent and would recognize him as a bear.

Rory shifted in the cave. "Did you see a cougar last night or this morning that you didn't know?"

"Yeah. Since I didn't know him, he didn't recognize me. I considered he could be a wild cougar, or someone new to town, and I didn't want to make him fearful of me. Is he lost? Are you searching for him?"

"We're taking him down, Blue," Rory said. "He's after my mate. This is Lacy."

"Your mate?" Blue smiled. "Congrats. I'll go with you."

Lacy wanted to ask why he was living in a cave when he was a shifter.

"Good. We can use your abilities too." Then Rory shifted.

Blue turned back into his bear. He was so much bigger than they were. But she was thrilled that he would help them.

She headed up the cliff further, and Rory stayed with her. Blue followed them. She'd read that bears could climb, but she thought he would be clumsier. He moved up and down the cliffs like a pro, just climbing rather than leaping as they did.

They continued searching for any sign of the cougar, exploring caves but not finding him. She wondered if he had returned to his clothes, wherever they were, dressed, then flagged down a car. Almost everyone would know to be on the lookout for Timothy. Unless the driver was a human, then he or she wouldn't know about it and might pick him up and take him into town.

Though she wondered if he wouldn't want to stay closer to the ranch where she was, maybe he thought there were too many people there to protect her. Where would he stay? Though he probably wouldn't realize cougars ran the whole town, and they were all watching out for her. But he had to stay somewhere.

It was too cold to remain in the woods or on the cliffs. He needed shelter and a warm fire, not to mention food and drink, unless he continued to wear his cougar coat.

He couldn't stay anywhere in town without the sheriff's department being alerted, but he wouldn't know that. If he tried to go to the motel where she and her granddad had stayed initially upon arriving in Yuma Town, Timothy would realize the owners were cougars. Maybe he wouldn't think they would know about him.

The alternative would be for him to stay in an abandoned building or an unoccupied home, if any were in the area.

They finally all gathered together. Hal indicated it was time to go home.

She figured it was lunchtime. They had been out there for hours. She was ready to get warm by the fire.

They all headed back to the ranch, and spread out again, but this time the bear went with them, to her amusement. Everyone was still searching for any sign that Timothy had gone this way after they had passed this location, looking for him.

Once they reached the ranch, Hal and the other law enforcement officers went to the main house to shift and dress.

Everyone else, including the bear, went into the bunkhouse.

The cougars all shifted and dressed, and then Rory said to Blue, "Go into my room, and you can shift and dress. We'll make lunch."

Blue grunted and then headed for Rory's room.

"What should we eat for lunch?" Lacy asked.

"We'll make mini pizzas. Everyone gets involved in making their own, adding the ingredients they want."

"That sounds good." Lacy looked in the fridge for cheese, bell peppers, black olives, and onions while Rory brought out the boxes of mini pizzas. Some of them had pepperoni. Some sausage or hamburger. Some just cheese.

"Pepperoni for you, right?" Rory asked Lacy.

"Yeah."

The other guys joined them and began adding their toppings while the oven preheated.

Blue finally entered the kitchen. "I'll take one of the hamburger ones, if that's all right with everyone."

"It sure is," Rory said. "We've got plenty for everyone. Just add the toppings that you want. We have cherry tomatoes on the counter over there. So what were you doing out there?"

"Girlfriend troubles. You know how it goes."

"Yeah, you met my last girlfriend, so you know I understand completely."

"I remember. But this one is the right one, I can tell."

"We're mated," Rory said.

"Well, hell," Wyatt said. "How long were you going to keep the secret from us?"

"Not long," Rory said.

The guys all slapped him on the back, and then they gave Lacy hugs.

"Do the Havertons know?" Blaze asked.

"Hal does. I'm sure Tracey knows now," Lacy said, adding cheese, olives, bell pepper, and tomatoes on her pizza.

"So what's the deal with the cougar you were trying to track down?" Blue asked.

"He's a stalker ex-boyfriend," Lacy said.

The oven dinged that the temperature was correct. Rory put all the pizzas in the oven and set the timer for seventeen minutes.

Then they all went into the living room and sat on the plush couches and recliners.

"What do you plan to do with him?" Blue asked.

"End his stalking," Rory said. "Permanently. There's no other way to handle this. The guy isn't giving up on Lacy, and we can't allow him to hurt or kill her."

"No, I don't blame you," Blue said, the other guys all agreeing.

"So if we can't find him out here, would a human have given him a ride back into Yuma Town?" Lacy asked.

"Possibly," Rory said.

"Okay, I had another thought. He needs food, water, and shelter. Is there somewhere he could go, like abandoned buildings? Or unoccupied homes if someone is trying to sell or rent a place?" Lacy asked.

Rory got on his phone. "Hey, Hal. Lacy proposed a couple of thoughts." Then he told him what she had said. He put the call on speakerphone.

"I'll tell Dan. They'll coordinate a search of any buildings that he might try to occupy," Hal said. "Dan and the others are having lunch with Tracy, the kids, and me. I'll let you know what they decide to do. What's Blue doing here?"

"Girlfriend trouble like usual."

Hal chuckled. "Okay, hope he gets it resolved soon."

The oven timer beeped, and Rory pulled out the pizzas. The other guys began bringing glasses of water to the table.

Rory cut the miniature pizzas into quarter-slices, and everyone grabbed their plates and carried them over to the table.

"I'll clean up. I know you guys have chores to do," Lacy said, once they finished eating.

"I'm going home," Blue said. "Thanks for lunch."

"Thanks for helping us out, Blue." Rory kissed Lacy as the guys headed outside. "We have some business to take care of."

She smiled.

Then Blue came out of Rory's bedroom as a bear, and Rory opened the front door for him so he could leave. "See you later. Good luck with your girlfriend."

Blue grunted, licked his hand, and then he went out the door, and Rory closed it. Rory lifted Lacy in his arms and headed for the bedroom with her.

She was ready.

9

F lorence couldn't wait to attend the Christmas dance with Frank. She'd always enjoyed going to them and dancing with anyone who wanted to dance with her, but she was really excited to do it with her mate, making everything so much more special.

She and Ava were finishing up the last of the orders at the coffee shop. They just had a couple of humans eating in there. The cougar customers had gone home to dress for the Christmas dance. Nina was watching over her sister and Florence still, just in case Timothy showed up there.

"I keep feeling he's close," Ava said, as they cleaned up the kitchen.

"Yeah, me too," Nina said.

"Timothy?" Florence asked.

"Yeah," the sisters both said.

"So he has returned to Yuma Town?" Florence asked as the last couple thanked them and left the shop. Florence wished them a merry Christmas.

"Maybe. Or he plans to," Ava said.

Florence turned off the Christmas music. She left some of the shop lights and the outdoor lights on. Then the ladies left the shop, locking the door. She headed home, with Nina following behind her to make sure Florence arrived safely, while Ava headed to her own place.

Once they reached Florence's house, Frank greeted her, hugging and kissing her.

Florence hugged and kissed him back. Nina waved goodbye and left to go home to get ready for the dance.

Florence loved this part of coming home now. A warm fire was going on in the fireplace, Christmas music was playing, the Christmas lights were all on, and Frank was dressed to party.

"You look handsome."

"Thanks. I'm ready for the dance."

"Me too. I'll go up and change clothes." She was soon dressed in a red wool dress, boots, and grabbed her faux white fur coat.

He smiled when he saw her. "You are beautiful and very sexy. Just perfect."

She smiled and felt like she was ready to walk on the red carpet with the man of her dreams. Even though they had disagreed about cases that they had worked on together, they had both had great ideas, and they'd solved their cases. But as a mate, he was perfect.

They drove over to the community center, where it was decorated with Christmas lights, a Christmas tree, garland, and red bows. Travis waved goodbye to them and then met up with his mate, who had brought him a change of clothes so he could enjoy the dance with her.

While they were there, they didn't need to have anyone watching out for them, which Florence was grateful for. She looked around but didn't see Lacy or Rory there yet.

They got some punch and a slice of angel food cake each. The cake was covered in chocolate and miniature sugar candy canes, making it spongy and crunchy, chocolate and peppermint all at the same time. Once they finished eating and drinking, they began dancing again.

Frank held her close during the waltzes, and she felt so connected with him. She was so in tune with him that she didn't even see when Rory and Lacy had arrived.

But then Rory and Lacy bumped into them in playful fun on the dance floor. They switched partners so that Rory could dance with Florence and Lacy could dance with her granddad.

Florence told Rory, "I mated Lacy's granddad." She knew that Frank would tell Lacy.

What she hadn't expected was for Rory to say, "That's great. Lacy and I have also mated."

Florence was thrilled. "That's wonderful."

"I'm so glad you and Frank mated too."

But that's not all she wanted to talk about. "Did you search for Timothy?"

"Yeah, with the ranch hands, our foreman, the sheriff, and deputies from both the sheriff's office and agents of the CSF, and Lacy as cougars, for the most part. We even found a bear shifter in a cave, and he helped us search. But we didn't find any sign of Timothy."

"Blue?"

"Yeah, girlfriend problems again."

Florence shook her head. "Ava and Nina said they kept feeling like Timothy was close to the coffee shop."

"Lacy mentioned he might have gotten a ride from humans to return to town. But he has to be staying somewhere then and getting food. It's too cold to be out in this weather as a human."

"That would make sense, but Lacy isn't in town any longer, except to attend special events. I keep feeling he'll want to stay nearer to where she is, but we have quite a number of people there to protect her," Florence said.

"Right. Which could mean he could be after Lacy's grandfather to get to Lacy, figuring that Lacy is too well protected at the ranch."

Before Florence could ask Rory any more questions, Lacy and Frank joined them to switch partners. But before they did, they congratulated each other on being mated cougars.

"I'm so thrilled for you," Lacy said, brightly smiling. She was wearing a slinky, sparkly red dress and looked beautiful.

"We're so thrilled for the two of you also," Florence said, giving her another hug. When she had hired Lacy at the coffee shop, she had never expected to gain a granddaughter of her own. She loved it. "Christmas at our house?"

"Yes. And Christmas Eve at the ranch?" Lacy asked.

"That would be great," Florence said.

Then they all got some more punch, and after they finished it, returned to the dance floor.

It didn't take long before Dan stopped the music. "During this most special of holiday seasons, we want to welcome two new cougars to our Yuma Town family. And we want to congratulate Frank and Florence for mating each other, and Rory and Lacy for having become mated cougars also."

Everyone clapped and cheered them. Then they came over to congratulate them with hugs.

Florence was glad everyone knew about their matings and was so happy for them. After all the congratulations, they began to dance again. This was the best Christmas holiday ever.

FRANK HELD Florence close as they waltzed the night away. They danced to faster dances too, but they preferred nice and slow and close. Some of the partygoers were leaving the dance a little early because they had younger kids at home with caregivers. But Frank and Florence stayed until closing.

When Shannon announced the end of the dance and reminded everyone of the Christmas bazaar tomorrow, Frank, Florence, Rory, and Lacy hugged each other to say goodbye.

Hal and Tracey followed Lacy and Rory home, but so did the other ranch hands, and Ted and Stella, who had all been enjoying the dance.

Then Travis and Bridget followed Frank and Florence home. He would stay the night with them while Bridget drove home to relieve the babysitter who was watching their twin boys.

"Do you want me to take you to the Christmas bazaar tomorrow?" Frank asked as they retired to the master bedroom.

Florence untied his tie. "Yeah, that would be fun. I need to get something for you, Lacy, and Rory for Christmas."

"Yeah, I was thinking about that too. Maybe we could go in together to get something for Rory and Lacy. They'll be starting anew. Maybe something warm for them since Lacy was living in the south and won't have wool blankets."

"Maybe we could get them a gourmet set of pots and pans. Lacy took off without being able to take anything much with her," Florence said. "Rory and the other guys also cook, but when Rory and Lacy have a place of their own, they'll need their own equipment."

"A good set of knives too," Frank said, getting into this.

She smiled. "When they marry, we'll check out their wedding list to see what else they need."

"What about us? I mean, do you want a justice-of-the-peace marriage? Or—"

Florence laughed. "Believe me, the cougar community will want to be involved."

Frank got a call on his phone. "It's Lacy. Yeah, are you okay?"

LACY AND RORY were sipping cocoa while they discussed their marriage after the first of the year. "Now, this is totally up to you, but what do you think about us having a double marriage ceremony with Mrs. Fitz and Granddad?" Lacy asked.

"I like the idea. The same people would be coming to both, and since we all mated at the same time, I think it would be nice to have it together."

"I was afraid since they've already each been married once, they might not want to have a fancy wedding, but they deserve it," Lacy said.

"Yeah, I agree."

"Okay, well, I'll call Granddad and tell him what we want to do." She got on her phone and put it on speaker when her grandfather answered her.

"What's going on?" her grandfather asked, sounding concerned.

"We're at the bunkhouse having cocoa. The guys all went to bed so we could have some alone time in the living room. We have a proposal we wanted to make about our wedding. I have this on speakerphone."

"I'll put my phone on it also. What do you have in mind?"

"We would like to have a double wedding with you all. Everyone would be coming to both, so it would be easier to have everyone go to one, don't you think?" Lacy asked.

Frank laughed. "We were just talking about that. We wanted to see if that would work for you."

"Well, that works for us."

"Us too," Mrs. Fitz said. "What is the home situation for the two of you?"

"Hal said he would give us land to build a house on. We need to decide on architectural plans, so that's our next step."

"Oh, that's wonderful. So when do you want to get married?" Mrs. Fitz asked.

"We need to see if we can schedule the community center, have a minister lined up, and decide on wedding clothes," Lacy said. "But we were thinking the end of May."

"All right. Have you planned a honeymoon yet?"

Lacy looked at Rory.

"Belize? They have cougars there so we could blend in while we take runs in the wilderness," Rory said.

"Belize it is," Lacy told her grandfather and Mrs. Fitz. "What about you two?"

"What about Oregon?" Mrs. Fitz asked.

"Sounds good to me," Frank said. "We can go to the Oregon Coast and stay at a cabin."

"Red wolves came through here last year and stopped in the coffee shop," Mrs. Fitz said. "They said they have cabins they rent on the coast."

"Shifters, great," Frank said. "We'll book one of them then."

"We're going to the Christmas Bazaar tomorrow. Will you be there?" Rory asked.

"Yeah, we're going," Mrs. Fitz said.

"Why don't we have lunch together? They'll have food booths available, and we can pick what we want," Rory said.

"Absolutely, that would be fun," Mrs. Fitz said.

"Okay, well, we'll get together tomorrow. Rory has to work early, then he can be off afterward to go to the bazaar. The guys are all giving him a hard time." Lacy loved him for wanting to take her. "Hal is taking his wife and the kids. Ted is taking Stella and his. That way we will have enough protection."

"That sounds good. We could all enjoy lunch together then," Frank said.

Then they ended the call, and Rory put their empty cocoa mugs in the dishwasher, swept her up in his arms, and carried her to bed.

~

FRANK AND FLORENCE cuddled in bed. "I'm glad we all get along." Frank was so relieved that Lacy had come around as far as the event that had torn them apart, and that she was thrilled he had mated Florence. It was something he had worried about in case she felt he was forgetting his mate's memory, but he wasn't. Just like he knew Florence wasn't forgetting about hers.

They just had a new lease on life when they met up and fell in love. He wished that Timothy wasn't still an issue though.

10

F lorence was up early, looking for gifts to buy online for Lacy and Rory. She'd already bought some things for Frank for Christmas. She just hoped everything would arrive on time. She heard Frank coming down the stairs. Travis was on his phone, trying to get an update on Timothy.

"So what do you think about these items for Lacy and Rory?" She showed her phone to Frank.

"Yeah, perfect. Let me put them on my card." Then he bought them.

"Will we put our money together?"

"Yeah, whatever you want to do. I'm fine with it."

"Okay. I'll put your name on the deed. I don't want to change the coffee shop's name because everyone knows it like it is." She headed to the kitchen to make breakfast and put together breakfast tacos while he made their coffee.

"I'm good with that."

"I do want to take your last name for my own. I'm just old-fashioned like that."

He smiled. "I'm glad. I'll be proud for us to be known as Mr. and Mrs. Everest."

She figured he would be, and if that made him happy, she was pleased.

Travis left the living room and said good morning to Frank. He began getting them glasses of water.

Frank brought over their mugs of coffee, then set the table.

"They haven't had any luck in finding anyone matching Timothy's description," Travis said. "Everyone is still on the lookout for him."

"I wanted to end this with him, but what if he left here for good, figuring he couldn't get to Lacy and it was too hard keeping a cover?" Florence asked.

"It could be, but he seems to be too obsessive. If he can do this to one woman, he can do it to others," Travis warned. "Plus, we don't want the situation to escalate. And Lacy would always be looking over her shoulder. So it would be better if we could terminate him and stop the problem."

"I agree," Florence said.

"Yeah, that's the best solution," Frank agreed.

They ate their breakfast tacos in silence.

"Are you going to open the coffee shop today?" Frank asked.

"Nah, the shops and eateries are closed in town so everyone who wants to can attend the bazaar and eat there. That way, there's no competition for the Christmas bazaar on that day."

"Oh, that's cool. It's great having a unified cougar-run town."

"It truly is. Everyone supports everyone else."

Then Travis got a call. "Yeah, Dan. Near Hal's ranch?" He glanced at Florence and Frank. "What? That's impossible." He drank the rest of his coffee. "Is it all right for them to go to the bazaar? Okay. Somebody's got to be mistaken. Yeah. Okay, I'll tell them. I guess Lacy and Rory and everyone out at the ranch have been alerted." He sighed deeply. "Good. Talk to you later."

"What's wrong now?" Frank refilled everyone's coffee mugs.

"We've had two different people see Timothy—one near the

coffee shop, and one near Hal's ranch this morning, both at the same time."

"So someone's wrong." Florence sipped her coffee.

"Or there are two of them. Identical twin brothers. They would smell the same and look the same. And if they're close to each other, they might have come out here together to track Lacy down." Frank got on his phone. "Hey, Lacy, does Timothy have an identical twin brother?" He put the call on speakerphone.

"He never said anything about him, if he had one. But Dan said that Timothy was spotted in two different locations at about the same time, so unless someone was mistaken and the one sighting wasn't of him, it might be that he has an identical twin brother. They're running together, or have separated forces," Lacy said.

Florence was on her phone in a flash, looking up Timothy to see what she could learn about him. "Oh, he works with him in the same PI agency. His name is Manning. It's on their website. He looks just like the picture you shared of Timothy." That was a real problem. Now they had two to deal with, if both sightings were correct.

So who had hurt Frank? Timothy or Manning?

"Well, the PI agency is going to lose both of their PIs over this," Travis said.

"He shouldn't have involved his brother," Lacy said. "I can't believe he never mentioned him. Maybe he was afraid I would fall for him instead."

"Maybe you dated both of them," Frank said.

Florence had thought the same, but she wouldn't have mentioned it, afraid she would upset Lacy. She frowned at Frank. He shrugged.

"Oh, I don't want to even think of that," Lacy said.

That would make Timothy an even worse boyfriend.

"We're still going to the bazaar," Lacy said. "This isn't going to stop us."

"I agree," Florence said. "We'll just have to be doubly diligent."

Then they finished the call, and Florence said to Frank, "I can't believe you told Lacy she might have been dating both of the brothers."

"She might have."

"But you know how distressing that would be?"

Frank shook his head. "Yeah. I was thinking of the possibility. I wasn't thinking about how upsetting that could be to her. I'll apologize to her when we see her at the bazaar."

"All right." Florence appreciated that he could see that he might have been a little indelicate in his comment. *Men.* He was thinking like an FBI agent without considering who he was talking to.

Rory hugged Lacy. "I'm sure you didn't date both brothers. Not when Timothy is so obsessed with getting you back."

"I don't know. I'm beginning to think I didn't know him at all."

"Well, true, since you didn't know he had a twin brother who worked with him in the same detective agency. They would have to be pretty close if his twin is out here helping him to get you back. He would have had to leave his job too."

"And from the look of it," Lacy said, reading over the site, "they own it. So no one is in charge for now."

"I agree. I'm off to work until we drive into town for the bazaar. What are you going to do?"

"Look for house plans. When you return, we can consider them. We can show Granddad and Mrs. Fitz and see what they think also."

"All right. That sounds good." Rory kissed her, then pulled on his jacket, gloves, and cowboy hat. "I'll see you in a little bit."

A house was a big deal. She hoped they would agree on a floor plan.

Then she sat in front of the fireplace, the fire crackling, the Christmas tree lights on, and began searching for house plans, hoping she would find something easy to love.

But she kept going back to the idea that she might have been dating Timothy's brother instead of Timothy. That was a really gross thought. Then again, would he have given her up to see his brother? As much as he was consumed with having her in his life, she didn't really think so.

If both brothers were out here trying to grab her, that would make it worse as far as trying to keep herself and her family safe.

Then she found a home design she really liked. It had three bedrooms and three baths upstairs, a guest room on the bottom floor with its own bathroom, a three-car garage, a recreation room, a den, a great room, a large kitchen, and a mud room—all great for kids, and if Granddad and Mrs. Fitz came to see them, they could stay overnight in the guest room. They could even live with them if they couldn't manage to live on their own as they got older.

When Rory came in, she went to hug him, but he said, "I've got to wash up first. I'll be right out."

"Here's a house plan I really like." She showed him the floor plan and pictures of one built to specifications. She couldn't wait to show it to him to get his opinion.

He looked it over. "Yeah, I like that. Lots of room for kids and your grandparents."

She hadn't thought of calling Mrs. Fitz her grandmother. She wondered how she would feel about it.

"Let's get Hal's approval on the plans, and we'll get his approval for a spot to build the home on, order the plans, and get a contractor. We'll probably have to wait until spring to start on the house when the snow melts so they can pour concrete."

"That sounds great."

He leaned over and kissed her, but wouldn't hug her. "I've got to clean up."

"Okay, see you in a few minutes."

"Are you ready to go to the bazaar?"

"I sure am."

"Hal and Tracey are ready too."

Then he hurried off to the bedroom, grabbed some clothes, and took a shower.

When he was all fresh, they made sure that Hal and Tracey were ready to go at the same time.

They drove into town, watching for any trouble, but not seeing any sign of either Timothy or Manning, just Hal and Tracey, they ended up at the bazaar at the big community center. Food stands and various crafts were offered.

Everyone had something different to sell. Christmas candles, Christmas candle holders, bowl and plate cozies, placemats, table runners, bibs, Christmas stockings, catnip toys, sweaters and snow booties for dogs, quilts and afghans, sherpa throws, gift packs, painted ornaments, braided and latch hook rugs, jars of spices, honey, soaps, magical winter silhouette lanterns, and tons of other items. Some of the items were geared for Christmas, while some were just for any time of year.

Mrs. Fitz also had a booth that Ava was managing with all kinds of desserts on display.

She had already bought some things for Rory, her grandfather, and Mrs. Fitz for Christmas. She hoped to find some stuff for Hal and Tracey for taking her in.

They soon saw her grandfather and Mrs. Fitz and joined them. "We'll meet up with you to eat at noon, all right?" Lacy asked them.

"Yeah, that will be great," her grandfather said.

"I have to do some last-minute Christmas shopping."

"Us too," Mrs. Fitz said.

Then they separated to search for gifts they wanted to buy. "I want to get something for Hal and Tracey for opening their home to me also," Lacy said.

"These lanterns are pretty neat. They could set them on their porch." Rory picked one up and looked it over.

"How many do you think?"

"Six."

She bought them, and he carried them out to the car. Perfect. She purchased a sherpa blanket for Rory that featured a couple of cougars snuggling and left it with her grandfather so Rory wouldn't see it. Her grandfather carried it out to his car. Dan went with him to give him protection.

It took Rory forever to rejoin Lacy, and she wondered if he had been shopping for her! And then took the gift out to the car. It was fun buying gifts in secret, but it was hard to do when the recipient was right there. He was smiling mischievously so she figured she had it right.

They looked at handmade wool sweaters, matching blue ones for Mrs. Fitz and her grandfather. Both were blue-eyed and wore a lot of blue.

Rory thought they were great, and after she paid for them, he took them out to the car. Then it was time to eat lunch and figure out what they wanted. Tables were set out for customers to eat at.

They joined her grandfather and Mrs. Fitz to decide on a meal. German sausage, Christmas tree pizza slices, meat pies, whole baked potatoes, mulled wine, crepes, stuffed mushrooms, tacos, enchiladas, and lots of desserts.

"I'm going to get a German sausage and baked potato with the works," Rory said.

"Cheese and broccoli crepe for me," Lacy said.

Mrs. Fitz ordered a beef pot pie and stuffed mushrooms. Lacy's grandfather got Swedish meatballs, green beans, and mashed potatoes. Then they all took a seat at one of the tables.

"Did you get everything you wanted?" Mrs. Fitz asked.

"I think so. What would you like to eat for Christmas Eve dinner?" Rory asked. "I was thinking we could have a rib-eye roast."

"Yeah, that would be great," Lacy's grandfather said.

"I would love that," Mrs. Fitz said.

"Me too," Lacy said. It sounded delicious.

"Turkey for Christmas Day? Or ham? Or both?" Mrs. Fitz asked.

"Ham?" Rory asked.

"That works for me," Lacy said.

They decided ham would be perfect, and figured out who would make which sides.

"We'll come over after I do chores in the morning," Rory said.

"That's perfect. Do you want to have breakfast with us? I could make cinnamon rolls," Mrs. Fitz said.

"Perfect." Her grandfather had a real sweet tooth.

"I love them," Lacy said.

"I do too," Rory said.

They finished their lunch. Lacy showed the house plans to her grandfather and Mrs. Fitz, and they loved them. Then everyone went home.

"We need to talk to Hal and Tracey about our house plans and learn where we can put the house." Lacy wished they could start on it right away! But at least the other ranch hands were giving them some privacy when they needed it. And she got a kick out of when they all watched a movie together and had buttered popcorn. The guys' comments about what was going on in the movie were hilarious. She was used to sitting quietly through a movie, laughing, or maybe shaking her head at dumb things people did.

So she found it fun to hear all their jokes about things, or to hear them tell what was wrong with some scenario or another.

"I'll call them." Rory got on Bluetooth and called Hal. "We found a house plan we really like. We'll show it to you, and you tell us if it's okay to build on the ranch. And where can we put it when spring is here?"

"Absolutely," Hal said. "Can't wait to see it. Come by the house once we all get home."

"We'll help you with anything you need," Tracey said.

"Thanks, we appreciate it." Lacy really hoped that they would approve the house plans.

When they reached the ranch, they went to Hal and Tracey's house to show them the house plans.

"Ooh, I love those," Tracey said.

"I do too. It's perfect for the ranch," Hal agreed.

Lacy breathed a sigh of relief.

Rory smiled and rubbed her back. "Thanks. We can't wait to build."

"We totally understand," Hal said. "It's hard to have much privacy at the bunkhouse for a mated couple. Ted and Stella felt the same way until they had their house built. We both have spare guest rooms, so if you think you would have more privacy that way, we are willing to let you stay with us."

"I'm fine with the way it is now. The guys are good about letting us have some time alone when we need it," Lacy said. If they moved in with Hal and Tracey, they had kids. She loved them, but they weren't conducive to romancing a mate.

With the house plans approved, she and Rory thanked them and headed to the bunkhouse for the night.

Rory hugged her. "Hal and Tracey are the best."

"They are."

"I've got to get something out of the truck, but you can't see it."

She chuckled. "Okay. I'll take a shower and—"

"Not without me."

She smiled and kissed him. "All right. I'll meet you in the bedroom in a few minutes."

She heard Rory talking with Wyatt and figured he was hiding her gift in his room. And then Rory barged into their room. "Shower time. And then dinner."

11

W hen Leyton, Frank, and Florence arrived at her house, they walked in through the garage door and saw the Christmas tree down, the ornaments smashed.

"Not again," Frank said, taking hold of Florence's hand and squeezing it to comfort her.

Her heart and his were pounding with anger.

Leyton was on his phone with Dan right away. He put it on speakerphone and told him what had happened.

"Don't search the house. Some of us will be there right away," Dan said.

"Timothy or his brother has been here. Or both of them," Leyton said.

Frank wanted to check the rest of the house to make sure no one was still inside. But after being put in the clinic the last time, he did what Dan told him to do.

Frank took pictures of the mess, but then he and Florence began cleaning up the broken ornaments.

Leyton ended the call and began helping them. "I guess we're going to have to put someone on the house even when you're not here."

"We've got the new security videos up," Florence suddenly said.

Frank had forgotten all about them.

They checked the videos and saw two men there, both with blond, curly hair and beards, stocky builds, and brown eyes, who looked like carbon copies of each other.

"Timothy and Manning," Frank said. "So now we have confirmed that both are here."

Dan arrived with Chase and Stryker. "Hell, what's wrong with these bastards?" Dan asked.

"Timothy hates Christmas. Maybe his brother does too," Frank said.

"Or maybe they're just mad that they can't reach Lacy, and they're showing their frustration since I'd taken her in at first." Florence put another broken ornament in the trash bag.

Shannon and Dan's wife, Addison, showed up with ornaments to replace the ones on the tree as the guys righted it. Only this time, they were beautiful, gold-embroidered balls with Styrofoam centers, gold acorns, wooden rocking horses with yarn tails and manes, and Victorian papered and shellacked balls with little gold ribbon ties. All were non-breakable.

Florence smiled. "What do I owe you?"

"Nothing. We've been gathering non-breakable ornaments since your last catastrophe," Shannon said, "just in case it happened again."

"Well, they're beautiful." Florence began hanging the new ornaments.

The ladies and Frank pitched in while the other guys searched the house and cleared it. Then they all watched the video of the two men.

"How did they get in this time?" Dan asked.

"I don't know." But then, as Florence was looking at the video again, she frowned. "They went through the front door. They must have used a lockpick."

"You don't have a key hidden out front?" Dan examined the door lock.

"No. I've never done that. You and a couple of others have keys to my house in the event of an emergency."

"Whenever you're both gone, we'll need to put someone on the house then," Dan said.

"Are we going to track them down?" Frank asked.

"Yeah."

"I'm going too," Florence said.

Shannon looked at Chase, her expression saying she didn't think Florence should go.

Frank didn't want Florence to go either. He wanted to, but he wanted to keep her safe even more. "I'm fine with staying here and protecting the tree."

Florence smiled. "All right. I'll stay here with you."

"And me," Addie said.

"I'll be going home." Shannon grabbed her purse to go.

"Thanks again for the beautiful ornaments. They'll be perfect for when Lacy and Rory have kids," Florence said.

Frank agreed.

Then Shannon hugged them and left.

The men all started their search outside while Frank and Florence started dinner. "Grilled ham and cheese sandwiches?" she asked.

"Yeah, that sounds good."

"I can't believe they were able to break into the house using a lockpick," Florence said.

"I agree. Especially since they broke a second-story floor window the last time." Frank brought out the bread.

Florence pulled the butter, cheese, mayonnaise, mustard, and ham out of the fridge. "Would you like one too, Addie?"

"No thanks. I'm going to have dinner with Dan once he returns."

"Okay." Florence buttered the bread slices, then put shredded cheese on one side of each, then coated the other slice with mayonnaise and mustard, and covered it with ham. Then she started cooking them.

Once the cheese started to melt, she flipped the ham side onto the cheese side to form the sandwich, then grilled it until both sides were browned.

She served them up while Frank poured mulled wine and added pickles and potato chips to each plate.

"Hmm, those look good," Addie said.

"Are you sure you don't want one?"

"No, really, I'm eating with the family when I leave here."

They ate their meal and then cleaned up. Then they checked outside to see if they could spot any of the guys. There were all kinds of footprints in the snow. They couldn't distinguish between Timothy and Manning's boot prints and Dan and the others who came in after them.

They went back inside, had hot cocoa, and watched a movie with Addie until the men returned.

"They took off through the woods behind your home, Florence," Dan said, hugging Addie, then kissing her on the cheek. "They finally reached a road and must have driven off. Which makes us believe they had two cars. We confiscated the one, but they're still able to move about in another vehicle."

"Unless they stole someone's car," Florence said.

Dan shook his head. "If they had, I'm sure it would have been reported."

"True," Florence agreed.

"I'll stay the night," Chase said.

"Nina will go with Mrs. Fitz to the shop tomorrow for protection. I'll relieve her halfway through the day," Addie said.

"Call me if you have any more trouble," Dan said, and he and Addie left in the same car she'd arrived in.

Stryker told them goodnight and left.

Florence offered Chase a grilled ham and cheese sandwich, and he ate it while she and Frank served up slices of pecan pie. Once Chase had eaten his sandwich, she cut him a slice of the pie as well.

"This is great," Chase said. "I'm so sorry you're having all these problems with the two men, and we can't stop them."

"We will." Florence sounded sure of it.

"Is your coffee shop open tomorrow for Christmas Eve?" Frank asked.

Florence served them all some milk. "It is. We'll close at five. Then we'll drive to Hal's ranch to spend Christmas Eve with Lacy and Rory."

"I could pick you up from the shop," Frank said.

"Sure, that would be great."

"We'll see who will be available to escort you to Hal's ranch," Chase said. "We'll also have someone stay at the house for when you return."

"That would be great." Florence carried the empty plates into the kitchen.

Frank soon followed with their milk glasses.

They cleaned up the kitchen and then helped make Chase's bed on the couch, though Florence told him he could stay in one of the guest rooms.

"I think I can be of more help if I'm downstairs, listening for anyone breaking in."

"Okay," Florence said, then she and Frank retired to the bedroom.

Frank wanted to go out and look for these men, figuring they were still nearby, but when Florence began removing his clothes, he smiled, and he had thoughts only of her.

FLORENCE LOVED that Frank came with her to the coffee shop for breakfast in the morning and even helped in the kitchen. He spilled flour and sugar on the floor, though he quickly cleaned it up, and burned a cheesecake while trying to figure out how to make a loaf of sourdough bread. But she loved that he was trying.

Sipping a peppermint mocha latte, Nina was sitting at one of the tables, watching for trouble while customers came in to purchase treats to go for their Christmas Eve dinners. A few came in for lattes and pastries for breakfast and were sitting at the tables nearby.

Finally, Frank left the kitchen, latte in hand, and joined Nina.

"Were you released from kitchen duty?" Nina asked.

In the kitchen, Florence smiled, overhearing the conversation with her cougar's hearing.

Frank chuckled. "When Florence made me a latte and said I could take a break, I figured she and Ava didn't need my help."

Nina smiled.

Frank cleaned up after patrons left the coffee shop. He planned to stay for the day.

Florence asked, "Which dessert should we bring with us to the bunkhouse?"

"If it doesn't sell, the chocolate cake with the Christmas tree and cougars on it? It's big enough to share with the rest of the ranch hands."

"Yeah, that will work." She put it in a box and set it aside.

"You don't want to see if you can sell it first?" Frank sounded surprised.

"Nope. It's ours. Did you pick out which dessert you want to take home with you, Ava?"

"The cupcakes with the reindeer on them," Ava said. "We're

having Nina and her family over for Christmas Eve, and that should be enough to satisfy everyone."

"All right. I was going to ask Nina what she wanted to take home with her."

"This will be enough. We don't want the kids or our husbands getting a sugar high," Ava said.

Florence laughed.

After they took turns eating lunch, they worked, Nina switching off with Addie for protection detail until closing.

Florence and Frank were already dressed in holiday sweaters and were ready to drive out to the ranch. She locked the door. Deputy Sheriff Ricky was waiting for them, while Ava and Addie headed to their own homes for Christmas Eve dinner. Ricky, Florence, and Frank drove to the ranch in two vehicles.

When they arrived at the ranch, Ricky returned home for his own dinner.

The ranch hands went to Stella and Ted's home for their dinner, but they would have dessert with Rory, Lacy, Frank, and Florence.

The fire was going in the fireplace, and the Christmas lights were all on. The aroma of rib-eye roast made Florence's mouth water. She didn't know what Wyatt and Blaze were going to eat at Ted and Stella's home, but they sure looked like they wanted to share some rib-eye before they left the bunkhouse.

"Everything smells delicious," Frank said.

"Yeah, I was thinking the same thing," Florence said as Rory carried the rib-eye roast to the table.

Lacy brought over mashed potatoes and gravy, and creamed spinach.

Florence gave everyone a glass of water. Frank opened a bottle of wine and poured a glass for each of them.

"Hal approved our house plan," Lacy told Florence and her grandfather.

"Oh, that's wonderful!" Florence said. "By the way, I know everyone calls me Mrs. Fitz, but I'm changing my last name to Everest, so everyone can call me Florence. Or you can call me grandma."

"Are you changing the name of the coffee shop?" Lacy asked.

"No. Everyone knows it by Fitz's Coffee Shop, so I'll leave it like it is."

"Saves on the cost of changing out all your signage," Rory said.

"That's exactly what I thought." Frank cut up some of his rib-eye roast. "This is so good."

"I agree." Florence took another bite.

"I love these and have them for the holidays whenever I can," Rory said. "They always have them at a reduced price for the holidays."

"Sounds like it should be a tradition for us to have," Lacy said.

"Right," Frank said.

Florence was all for it. "For Christmas, since you will be there also, I don't believe we need anyone else there to provide security."

"I agree," Rory said. "I'm deputized. And you and Frank are retired FBI agents, so we should be good for just the day."

"Granddad taught me how to shoot at the firing range. I just need a spare gun," Lacy said.

"I'll bring two guns with me," Rory said.

When they finished eating, they cleaned up, and then Lacy set up a hot cocoa bar, complete with mugs of hot chocolate, candy canes, whipped cream, marshmallows, and sprinkles, so everyone could make their own to go with their slices of chocolate cake.

Then Wyatt and Blaze returned to the bunkhouse to have dessert and cocoa with them.

"Man, that rib-eye roast sure smells good," Wyatt said.

"Yeah, maybe we can have one for New Year's Day," Blaze said.

"Oh, speaking of that, we'll be going to a New Year's Eve party," Florence said to Frank.

"More dancing? I'll be ready for it," Frank said.

After that, everyone agreed to watch a Christmas movie, and they started *A Christmas Story*.

When they finally finished the movie, they all said their good-nights, though Lacy was going to give some of the leftovers to Florence and Frank.

"Oh, no, just keep it. Wyatt and Blaze can snack on it. We'll have food tomorrow with leftovers," Florence said.

Wyatt and Blaze smiled, looking glad they were going to have some of the rib-eye roast after all.

"We'll escort you home," Wyatt said.

"Okay, sounds good." Florence grabbed her purse.

"You could stay here the night, and we could all go together," Lacy said.

"Yeah, Hal and Tracey or Ted and Stella would put you up," Blaze said.

Florence wanted to go home for the night so she could get things ready for Christmas tomorrow. But she looked at Frank to see what he wanted to do.

As if he knew what she was thinking, he took her hand and squeezed. "We need to prepare meals for Christmas."

She squeezed his hand back, telling him he had said the right thing, but she had been leaving it up to him. He would have done anything she wanted.

They hugged Rory and Lacy, Frank helped Florence into her coat, and he put his on. Then they left with their escort.

"It's more relaxing at the house with you," Florence said.

"I was thinking the same thing. And we still have someone watching the house, no matter if we are there or not." The car slipped on the ice, and Frank tightened his grip on the steering wheel.

"Exactly."

"Christmas Eve was a success."

"It was. I had such a nice time with Lacy and Rory," she said.

"Yeah. I'm so glad that Lacy is speaking with me again, and I really like Rory. I can tell they are really into each other."

"They are. Just like us."

Frank smiled. "Yeah." Florence was so charismatic and made him feel like he was everything. He hoped he made her feel like that's how he thought about her too.

All the way to Florence's house, Frank and Florence watched the mirrors for any sign of Timothy or his brother following them, but they didn't see anything out of the ordinary.

"Maybe they'll leave us alone for Christmas," Florence said.

"Or figure we won't be expecting them to hit the house on Christmas Day." He drove into the garage, then they got out and waved goodbye to Wyatt and Blaze.

They said, "Merry Christmas."

"Merry Christmas!" Florence and Frank said.

Travis came out of the house and waved at the ranch hands.

Then Frank closed the garage door, and they went inside to find the fireplace going. Everything looked so Christmassy and inviting. He was so glad that Travis was fine and the tree hadn't been turned over this time.

"We don't need anyone to stay with us tomorrow while Rory and Lacy are here for Christmas Day," Frank told Travis. "We all know how to use a gun, and Rory has a spare gun for Lacy."

"I'll be staying the night, and I'll talk to Dan to see what he wants to do about it. He has the final word," Travis said.

"All right." Frank understood that Dan didn't want to take any chances with their welfare. But the good thing about Florence's home was that it was close to town. So if they needed help, they would have assistance right away.

They helped him make up the bed on the couch, then retired to their room.

"Merry Christmas Eve," Frank said, kissing Florence.

She hugged him. "Merry Christmas Eve. This is the best one ever."

"I agree."

They changed into pajamas, climbed into bed, and cuddled together. Neither of them had wrapped any presents yet. They would have to do so in the morning.

"Do you get up early for Christmas morning?" Florence asked.

Frank chuckled. "I get up early all the time. But I haven't really celebrated Christmas since Lacy didn't want to see me."

"I'm so glad that's resolved and that you and I have each other."

"I am too. I couldn't be happier."

"I always eat at someone's home for Christmas Eve dinner and Christmas Day lunch, and whoever fed me would always give me something, and I would give them something for the special day."

"Well, now we have Lacy, Rory, and us, and if anyone else is alone for the holidays, we can take them in like the others took you in."

She snuggled against him and kissed him. "I agree."

They finally fell asleep when Frank's sleep was disturbed, and he swore he thought he heard reindeer walking around on the roof.

12

Florence was sound asleep when she felt Frank stir. He sat up in bed.

"Are you okay?" she asked. She thought if he were just going to the bathroom, he would have, but instead, he was staring up at the ceiling, listening, watching.

"I swore I heard reindeer on the roof."

She might have believed it was cute, but her first thought was of Timothy. What if he and his brother were up on the roof? "Timothy and Manning."

They both got out of bed and dressed. With guns in hand, they headed downstairs to wake Travis. He was sound asleep on the couch, but as soon as he heard them coming down the stairs, he sat up, his gun in hand.

"I didn't hear anything, but in his groggy state, Frank heard reindeer on the roof. Could it be Timothy and Manning?"

"Let's go check." Travis threw on his boots, and they all put on their coats.

They also pulled on hats and gloves, then armed, they headed out front. They had to reach the sidewalk to see the roof and if anything was on it. Nothing. Then they moved around to the back of the house and saw imprints on the snow-covered roof where the cougars had left their paw prints and had lain.

They also saw that the trellis they had removed from the house and put in the garden was leaning against the house, and the cougars must have climbed it to reach the roof. Cougars could leap between eighteen and twenty feet vertically, but the root was about twenty-five feet high.

They explored the area out back and saw fresh tracks the men had made that headed into the forest. Travis got on his phone. "Hey, Dan, Timothy, and Manning have returned. They were up on Florence's roof. But it appears they've taken off through the woods. They had been up on the roof as cougars. Uhm, yeah, they used that trellis we removed."

Travis glanced at Florence and Frank. "Not sure. It's hard to tell. They moved in a single file. They might have dressed and taken off as humans, but the path is narrow, so they might have traveled as cougars." He let out his breath as he stared at the trail.

Florence knew he wanted to go after the men, but he was stuck babysitting them.

"All right. See you in a few." Then Travis finished the call. "Dan wants us to return to the house. He and some of the others will look for the brothers."

Despite wanting in the worst way to go after the twins, Frank took Florence's hand, and they went back into the house. Travis followed behind them.

"I know you want to go after them, but we want to keep you safe," Travis said. "If anything were to happen to you, we would never forgive ourselves."

"I agree," Frank said, "but I do want to end this for certain."

"Yeah, we all do."

Then they gathered in the living room. They couldn't go to sleep until they had some word about the brothers.

"Do you want something to drink? Hot tea? Decaf?" Florence asked.

"Yeah, that would be good," Frank said.

"I'll have a cup," Travis said.

Florence made them all cups of tea, and then Dan and the others arrived—Chase, Chet, Ricky, Leyton, Stryker, and Hal.

"We're on our way," Dan said.

"Thanks," Florence said.

After drinking their tea and watching a movie to try and stay awake until Dan and the others returned, she and Frank were cuddling on the couch until they both fell asleep.

FRANK HEARD voices and realized he had fallen asleep on the couch. Florence was cuddled up with him and was still asleep. Travis was talking low to Dan in the dining room.

Dan shook his head at Frank, indicating they hadn't found the brothers. Then he waved to him, and he and the others left the house. Travis locked up after them.

Frank kissed Florence's forehead. She stirred and opened her eyes. Then she sat upright quickly. "Did they catch them?"

"No. They're going home. Are you ready to return to bed?" Frank asked.

"Yeah. Let's go." Florence yawned.

Travis said, "We're under winter weather warnings. We're going to have heavy snow on Christmas night. It might be better if Rory and Lacy stay the night with you."

Florence looked at her weather app. "Oh, no, a blizzard. We'll try to get them to stay the night."

Frank was disappointed that they still hadn't caught the brothers. He was glad he had heard them up on the roof, though. Maybe going after them again had convinced them they couldn't hurt him or Florence, given how many people were watching out for them.

He settled down with Florence in bed, hoping they could both get back to sleep. Before they knew it, it was time to wake; no more reindeer sounds on the roof, which had turned out to be cougars. Kittens had gotten on top of his roof and run across it one night when he lived in Florida, and he swore they sounded like a stampede of elephants. So he wasn't surprised when he heard the cougars, though he knew they would have been trying to be quiet.

"Breakfast?" Florence asked, not making a move to leave the bed.

"Yeah, sure." He got out of bed and started to dress. "Cinnamon rolls?"

"Absolutely." Then she finally climbed off the mattress and hugged and kissed him. "Merry Christmas."

He smiled. "Merry Christmas, honey."

Then she dressed, and they headed downstairs. Travis was gone. Leyton was there.

"What did Dan say about having someone stay here with us while Rory and Lacy are here?" Frank asked.

"He said it was fine since we're so close by. But after Christmas, if you two are alone, we'll have someone staying with you until we catch these guys."

"All right," Florence said.

Just then, Rory and Lacy arrived, wishing everyone a merry Christmas and giving hugs all around, even to Leyton.

"Merry Christmas, everyone. If you have any trouble at all, call us." Then Leyton left.

"The snow is really picking up," Lacy said.

"We want you to stay overnight." Florence motioned to the guest rooms upstairs. "Once the gifts are wrapped and under the tree, you can choose a room."

"All right, if it's terrible out, we will," Rory said.

Frank figured he knew he would be needed at the ranch, but he wouldn't risk Lacy's safety either by returning to the ranch during a blizzard.

Florence turned on the Christmas music, Lacy lit the cinnamon-scented candles, and Frank plugged in all the Christmas lights.

Lacy and Florence began making fresh cinnamon rolls while Frank made everyone coffee, and Rory worked on the eggnog topped with nutmeg. Then Lacy grilled some pork sausages to eat with their cinnamon rolls.

They were soon sitting down to breakfast, and Frank and Florence were telling about the reindeer on the roof that turned out to be cougars.

"Oh, no, I can't believe they keep coming here." Then Lacy frowned. "They probably thought I would be here last night for Christmas Eve."

"That's what I was thinking," Frank said.

"Me too." Florence drank some of her coffee. "Frank and I still need to wrap presents."

"We need to run out to the pickup truck and bring ours in," Lacy said.

"Okay, well, we're going to head upstairs and wrap up things and bring them down." Florence carried some of the mugs into the kitchen.

Lacy brought in some of the others.

Then Lacy and Rory left the house to gather presents, and Frank and Florence ascended the stairs to wrap theirs. Florence brought wrapping paper, Christmas bags, tape, and bows out of her closet and divided them between them. She had put Christmas presents in Lacy's guest room. Frank had used the other one to hide his gifts.

With arms full of wrapping and such, they entered the bedrooms and shut the doors. After a while, they carried the packages downstairs and put them under the tree.

"It looks like a lot of us were nice and not naughty," Lacy said.

Rory kissed her. "I'll say."

Lacy kissed him, then headed for the kitchen. "Coffee or cocoa for everyone?"

"Cocoa," Florence said.

"Same for me," Frank said.

"I'll help you." Rory went into the kitchen with Lacy, and the aroma of chocolate and sweet whipped cream filled the air.

When they sat down with their mugs of cocoa, they stared at the Christmas tree for a few minutes. Rory loved having family like this for Christmas. It wasn't the same as sharing Christmas with the ranch hands.

"Do one of you want to do the honors and play Santa?" Florence asked.

Rory glanced at Frank. Frank smiled. "I'll do some, and you can do some."

"Sounds like a deal."

Rory was glad that they wanted to get on with Christmas. They were having a blast. Opening gifts, loving what everyone got for them. They even had gifts in the Christmas stockings—treats, chocolate, mini jars of honey, beef jerky, and more.

Then Florence and Lacy started heating the cooked spiral ham.

Lacy washed her hands and hugged Florence. "I thank my lucky day that I met you, and my grandfather mated you."

Florence smiled. "I feel the same way."

Then they all went back into the living room and played Trivia and other games until it was time to make the sides for the ham, parmesan roasted asparagus, and mashed potatoes.

They sat down for lunch and began passing the sides around.

"I haven't had a real family in years," Rory said. "You all make this super special."

"I was going to say the same thing," Florence said.

"Well, I'm delighted that Lacy and I have expanded our family, and we hope it will continue to grow." Frank began slicing the ham.

Rory smiled at Lacy. Her cheeks were a brighter pink. Yeah, kids were on the agenda.

He had thought of offering to cut the ham, but Frank seemed to want the role as the senior male there, even though both Florence and Lacy cut up meat in their line of work also.

Once everyone's plates were filled, they began eating their Christmas lunch.

"Everything tastes great," Lacy said.

"I was thinking the same thing," Frank said. "Last year, I had takeout Chinese."

Florence smiled and reached over and squeezed his hand. "We can have anything you like for Christmas or Christmas Eve in future years."

"I agree," Lacy said. "Florence and I can make tasty Asian dishes if everyone wants something different next year."

"As long as we have turkey for Thanksgiving, I'm game," Rory said.

"Yeah, I prefer turkey also." Frank buttered another roll.

"What about New Year's Eve? We'll be going to the dance, but what about dinner before that?" Frank asked. "Steaks sound good to me."

Everyone agreed.

The wind was howling, and after they finished eating, they looked out the windows at the blizzard, a total whiteout, the wind whipping about at about eighty miles per hour.

"We're staying here the night." Rory wrapped his arm around Lacy's shoulders.

"Yeah, that's too dangerous to drive in," Florence said.

Rory wondered about the twin brothers and if they were out in this storm. Their thick winter coats would keep them warm, trapping air close to the skin. But they would also have to find a cave, rock overhang, or dense shrubs to protect themselves from the storm, and move to lower levels where it would be warmer.

If they were wild cougars, they would increase their body fat in wintertime. But for humans, they were often warmed up by fires or heating units, so that might not happen for shifters. The cougars also had higher body temperatures and, in conditions like these, could sleep more to conserve energy. Too bad they couldn't catch them while they were holed up somewhere.

"Does anyone want to watch *The Santa Clause*?" Florence asked.

"Yeah, I do," Lacy said.

So they watched the movie while Rory stroked his light beard, and the Santa kept trying to remove his white beard whenever it appeared.

They all loved how he was eating cookies and growing a belly like Santa's. When the movie was done, Florence said, "It's time to make 7-layer bars for dessert."

"I'll help," Frank said, before Lacy could offer.

"We're going to take our gifts up to the guest room we'll stay at." Lacy began gathering her gifts.

Rory quickly began cleaning up his gifts and heading upstairs with them. Lacy followed him while Frank spread chocolate chips on the 7-layer bars.

"This is really simple," Frank said.

"Yeah, it is. I usually make it to sell at the shop, but it's fun because there are four of us to enjoy it, especially since Lacy and Rory will be staying for another day. Though they can always take some home to share with the other ranch hands."

She put the baking dish in the oven and started the timer. "Twenty-five minutes to cook."

"Let's take our presents up to the room," Frank said.

Florence glanced at the half-wall on the second floor. She thought Lacy and Rory would have just left their presents in the guest room and come downstairs, but they were still up there.

Having a special Christmas moment? Florence smiled, hauled her gifts upstairs, and carried them down the hall to the master bedroom.

After she put them away, she helped Frank put his things away. Then they went back downstairs to carry all the Christmas treats into the pantry. They could have sampled some of those for dessert, but she really loved 7-layer bars, and it was the only time of the year that she made them.

Once they put away the rest of the Christmas treats, they sat down in the living room, and both looked up at the second story. Then they smiled at each other, kissed, and hugged.

"Youth," Frank said.

"Yeah, but we're going to do what they're most likely doing when we go to bed," Florence said. "The 7-layer bars had to cool down anyway before we can eat them."

"While upstairs things are heating up." Frank put his arm around her shoulders, and they leaned back on the couch and just cuddled.

13

L acy kissed Rory and smiled at him in bed in the guest room. She caressed his hair. "They'll be waiting for us."

"They will be. And they'll know what we've been up to."

"We're newly mated. It's Christmas."

"Agreed."

Lacy still felt slightly embarrassed to return to the living room. They dressed, and Rory embraced her. "You are turning red."

She laughed.

Then they went downstairs to join Frank and Florence and saw them snuggled together on the couch, sound asleep.

"That's so sweet," she whispered to Rory.

Smiling, he agreed.

She snapped a photo of them. "Their first Christmas together."

He took a picture of Lacy and himself in front of the Christmas tree. "Our first Christmas together."

Florence stirred, then her eyes shot open. "Oh, my, you caught us asleep."

Lacy smiled. "You deserved it after all that you did for everyone for Christmas."

"Even the guys and I take a catnap sometimes," Rory said.

"Oh, the 7-layer bars should have cooled down by now." Florence got up from the couch.

Frank did too.

"Does everyone want some? Or we can have some of the cookies and candies we got for Christmas." Florence went into the kitchen to cut up the 7-layer bars.

"I'm all in on the bars. Does anyone want milk?" Rory brought out some glasses.

"Milk for me," Frank said, everyone agreeing.

They all took their Christmas tree plates with the magic bars and glasses of milk to the table.

As soon as Lacy took a bite of hers, she moaned with pleasure. "Now these are so good. It has to be a family tradition from now on."

"I agree with Lacy. I've never had these before. They're great." Rory ate more of his.

"Decadent." Frank took another bite. "And so easy to make, even I can do it."

Lacy chuckled. "You're a good cook. You were just not used to the coffee shop's kitchen, oven temperature, and all the distractions."

They finished their magic bars and then cleaned up.

They checked out the windows. It was still snowing like crazy, with whiteout conditions a few feet out from the windows, and the wind still howling like an uncontrolled icy beast.

"I'm glad we're here," Lacy said, cuddling with Rory.

"Yeah, me too. The guys will give me grief when I get back for taking an extended work break over Christmas, but—" Rory squeezed Lacy.

"It couldn't be helped, and we're thrilled you're here," Florence said.

"We sure are," Frank said.

"I'm glad that no one else had to stay with us for protection. They would have been separated from their family until the blizzard ends, and we can unbury ourselves," Rory said.

The snow was piled up on the front porch halfway up the windows. It would be a bear to clear off the driveway, the porch, even Rory's pickup.

"Time for bed?" Rory asked.

"Yeah, it's time." Lacy was ready.

Frank and Florence headed for the stairs too. Florence turned off the lights downstairs, and they all went up the stairs.

"Merry Christmas," Florence said to everyone.

A chorus of "merry Christmas," followed.

Then they all retired to their respective bedrooms.

"That was a really great Christmas," Rory said.

"I agree." Lacy removed her clothes and climbed into bed.

Rory quickly joined her, and they were back to kissing and making love.

FRANK WOKE to find Florence had left the bed. It was four in the morning, but he didn't hear her in the bathroom or downstairs.

He put on the new green pajamas that Florence had gotten him, featuring a cougar in a Santa's hat, and a pair of furry slippers. Then he left the room and descended the stairs.

Wearing the blue penguin pajamas and blue fluffy slippers Frank had gotten her, she was staring out the front window.

He ran his hand over her back. "What's wrong?"

"The howling wind woke me. I...I thought I heard something else, but it was probably just the wind."

They moved into the kitchen and looked out the kitchen window. They didn't see anything but snow and more snow.

Then they moved to the den and peered out the windows,

looking for any sign of trouble, trees or branches down, but they really couldn't see anything.

He wrapped his arm around her waist. "We could go out there and look, but I don't think we would see much."

"I agree. We wouldn't see anything out there, and if we could even navigate the piles of snow, we could actually get lost in this mess."

"Do you want to go back to bed?"

Florence sighed. "Yeah, sure."

But he knew she was feeling unsettled about whatever she had heard. "You didn't hear reindeer on the roof, did you?"

She smiled at him. "No. As high as the wind has been, a branch could have torn loose and hit the house, then blown off, or been buried in the snow."

"That sounds reasonable."

Then they went back to bed and snuggled in their PJs. "Love your PJs," she said.

"Love yours too."

"They're perfect for wandering around the house when I think I'm hearing things."

"I must have just been sleeping really heavily," Frank said.

"Like I was when you heard the reindeer on the roof."

Florence wished she'd been more awake when she'd heard whatever she'd heard. Then she was wide awake, like Frank had been when he'd heard the cougars on the roof. Could the brothers navigate this blizzard and break into the home?

She couldn't fall asleep. She just kept listening to the wind blowing against the windows.

Frank was caressing her back, and she figured he was trying to help her fall asleep, or maybe he couldn't sleep now either.

But she loved how compassionate he was, and his touch was heaven.

Then she must have fallen asleep when she smelled coffee brewing in the kitchen. "I think the kids are up."

Frank kissed her cheek. "Yeah, smells like the coffee is ready."

They dressed and then headed downstairs.

Only Lacy was in the kitchen.

"Is Rory sleeping in?" Florence was incredulous.

"He's coming. He swore he heard something around four this morning outside the house."

"Oh, I did too." Florence couldn't believe it.

"Oh, no. I didn't hear a thing. I was sleeping too heavily."

"Me either," Frank said. "We looked out all the windows but couldn't see anything at all."

"The snow is still falling, and the wind is still blowing like crazy." Lacy poured them all mugs of coffee while Rory came down the stairs and joined them.

"Did anyone hear anything around four this morning?" Rory added sugar and cream to his coffee.

"I did. Frank didn't," Florence said. "What do you think it was?"

"A branch hitting the window?" Rory asked.

"I thought of it. We couldn't see anything."

"I went downstairs to check, but didn't see anything. I must have missed the two of you," Rory said.

"Yeah, we went back to bed."

"I did too, but couldn't get back to sleep," Rory said.

"Neither could we." Frank got them refills on their coffee.

"What do you want to eat for breakfast?" Florence asked.

"Ham and cheese omelets?" Lacy asked.

"That'll work." Florence got up to go into the kitchen, and Lacy hurried after her.

They ate their breakfast, then cleaned up the dishes.

Rory said, "I'm feeling housebound."

"I'm not sure we can get outside." Lacy gingerly opened the front door. The amassed pile of snow began to fall into the house, and Lacy quickly shut the door. "Sorry."

Florence and Frank came over and wiped up the melting snow.

"I'll check the back door," Rory said.

They all went that way, but the snow was packed up even higher against that door. It was so packed, it didn't fall into the house like the snow at the front door. He quickly shut the door and locked it.

"As high as the snow is, we could probably jump out of the second-story window and land safely," Rory said.

"And sink in it over our heads if the snow is too powdery soft. Then we would need a rescue team, and nobody is probably going to be able to get out in this weather for anything," Lacy said.

"What about the garage door? Snow will probably block it the same as the front door, but we can try it," Frank said.

They all headed out to the garage door.

Florence knew it would be just like the front door. Sure enough, as soon as Frank opened the garage door, they were faced with a wall of snow. Everyone got their phones out and took pictures for posterity.

"You can send that to Ted and Hal to show them how stuck we are," Lacy told Rory.

He smiled. "I imagine the ranch is in a similar situation. The guys are going to have a time feeding the animals, though the animals will all be in the barns for protection."

Frank closed the garage door. "I guess we're stuck here for a while. At least we have plenty of food and drink."

RORY HATED SHOWING his vulnerability in front of Lacy and the others, admitting he felt claustrophobic. Maybe he would feel better if he talked about it. "My issue with feeling claustrophobic gripped me when I was stuck in a cabin during a blizzard for a week. My parents were supposed to join me. I was eighteen at the time. They couldn't get to me, and I couldn't leave the cabin. I had no phone service during the ordeal. They were frantic about reaching me."

"Oh, that's horrible!" Lacy said as they went back to the living room and sat down on the couches. "What happened?"

"I had brought food I liked to eat, so I had enough food. I was fortunate that none of the pipes froze, or I wouldn't have had water. I was always used to being around people. I started working for Hal and Tracey when I was sixteen. And before that, I lived at home. So this was a vacation to spend with my family. It was Valentine's Day, and I didn't have a sweetheart. But we had the worst blizzard that year."

"Like this year?" Lacy asked.

"If this keeps up, it might be just as bad as that year," Florence said. "I was housebound for five days until some of the towns-people could clear the roads and my driveway. The snow had stopped, but the piles were so high, and it continued to be cloudy and cold, so it just wasn't melting."

"Exactly." Rory ran his hands through his hair. "The cabin was even farther out so it took work crews longer to reach me. Though everyone was trying to get to me."

"You have us this time," Lacy said.

Rory smiled. "Yeah, and I'm glad for that. I just figured if I could get out for a breath of fresh air, I would feel better."

"You could open one of the upstairs windows and just breathe in the fresh air until you feel less confined," Florence said.

"I'll go with you." Lacy took hold of Rory's hand. "Ready?"

"Sure." Even though they had opened doors and breathed in the fresh air, snow still walled them in, lending to that claustrophobic feeling. He didn't mind snow; he just didn't like confinement.

They headed up the stairs, and Florence said to Frank, "Are you all right?"

"Yeah. Being from Florida, I'm not used to it, but I'm here with you, and I feel fine."

"Good."

"What about you?"

"Oh, I can manage anything for a couple of weeks."

Lacy walked into the guest room that they weren't using so they wouldn't make their bedroom cold. Rory opened the window and breathed in the fresh, cold air, the wind still blowing, whistling through the trees, the snowflakes collecting on their hair, eyelashes, and his beard.

"Do you feel better?"

"Yeah," he said. "This feels great." He pulled her under his arm and just enjoyed the "freedom." Looking at the mountains of snow below them was a lot different than looking at it from the ground floor, seeing a wall of it keeping them from going anywhere.

He thought he heard something in their guest room, but he was surprised Florence or Frank would go in there instead of their own bedroom. He and Lacy hadn't picked up their clothes from undressing last night and hadn't made their bed, just being lazy. But he didn't want them to see that.

Lacy snuggled with him closer.

He knew he had closed the door before he went downstairs, but he didn't hear anyone open the door to the room to enter it.

He figured he was being paranoid. If the brothers were in their guest room, that meant trouble. Though if they'd broken the window again, surely, they would have heard it even from downstairs. Rory and the others couldn't call for help. They didn't have any signal on their phones. No one could help them in these conditions anyway. And his guns were in the living room.

"What's wrong?" Lacy asked him.

"I thought I heard someone in our guest room."

Lacy frowned. "I doubt Florence or Frank would have gone in there."

Rory closed the window as quietly as he could. Then he crossed the floor to the door. "I don't want to leave you here if the brothers are in our guest room. I want you downstairs with your grandfather and Mrs. Fitz."

"And you?"

"I'll be right behind you." Even though Lacy told Rory that she knew how to shoot a gun, she wasn't law enforcement. At least he was deputized, and Florence and Frank were retired FBI agents who had done lots of fieldwork.

"When you reach the living room, turn into your cougar."

Lacy hugged him. They didn't even know whether the brothers were in the guest room. But they had to prepare for the worst.

"They might not be there," he whispered to her.

She nodded. Then he opened the guest room door and instantly faced two men with guns—Timothy and Manning.

14

————

Frank heard the door to the guest room he had stayed in slam shut and lock. He glanced at the low wall and saw Timothy and Manning at the guest room door. Frank grabbed Florence and hurried her to the far end of the living room, where the brothers couldn't see them. Their hearts were pounding like crazy.

"Timothy and Manning are upstairs. I don't believe using the guns will be the way to go. We might not hit the brother closest to the wall, but we could easily miss at the angle we would have to shoot from."

"I agree," Florence said. "We have only one option for dealing with the brothers."

They both quickly yanked off their clothes, kissed and hugged, just in case they didn't make it out alive, and shifted.

They headed toward the stairs. If they ran up the stairs, they would make noise and alert the brothers, which was the reason they couldn't ascend them with guns readied for a better shot also. The stairs were ten feet high. As cougars, they could easily leap that distance to the top of the stairs. Frank was thinking he could jump onto the wall, which was three feet high, making the leap a total of thirteen feet. He would be closer to the one brother then and could pounce on him before he fired a shot at them.

One of the brothers shot at the lock on the guest room door. They had to stop the men before they reached Rory and Lacy. Frank was sure they would kill Rory and try to take Lacy with them. Ex-boyfriend stalkers could be unpredictable. They might just kill Lacy too.

The one man shot at the door lock again, and when that didn't work, he kicked the door in.

Frank took a running leap at the upper-floor wall, praying he would land on it correctly and not miss it or overjump it. He landed on the very top with precision like a young cougar. He still had it in him. He growled in his fiercest manner. Cougars silently hunted, but when aggravated or agitated, they would cry out, growl, or shriek. He couldn't help himself. He was madder than hell.

The brother closest to him whipped around. Everything happened so quickly after that. Florence leaped onto the wall next to Frank, and both pounced on the one brother that they could reach at the same time.

After the guest room door splintered, out came two cougars snarling and screeching, biting and clawing at the other brother. Florence and Frank might be older cougars, but they still had the fight in them, the adrenaline rushing through their veins, making them feel like much younger big cats.

Both brothers were trying to shoot the cougars, the bullets hitting the walls and ceiling. Lacy got hold of one of the brothers' wrists and bit hard, crushing the bones. He immediately dropped the gun.

Florence bit the other brother's right hand, having the same effect. Frank went for the brother's throat to end this now. If he didn't, they would have to hold them hostage until Dan could take them into custody, but the result would be the same. They would terminate them as dangerous as they were.

The one brother fell limply to the floor, and the other one did the same thing as Rory bit him in the throat.

Once the brothers were dead, the cougars were heaving with exhaustion, bloodied, but none had been shot. Frank only wished they could notify the sheriff's office.

He nuzzled Florence, and she licked his face and leaned against him. Lacy sat down next to Rory and rubbed her face against his. Then he and she went into the guest room where they had left their clothes. They shifted, washed up, and dressed.

Likewise, Frank and Florence ran down the stairs to shift, clean up, and dress.

"Are you all right, Lacy?" Rory asked.

"Yes. Relieved, horrified, but glad it's over with. We can't leave them in the house. The only thing we can do is shove them out the window into the snow and retrieve the bodies when the snow melts."

Lacy couldn't believe her grandfather and Florence could fight that well as older cougars. She was proud of them, but wanted to check on them after she and Rory got rid of the bodies. She couldn't believe how she didn't know which brother was Timothy and which was Manning. They were identical in every way. The only thing that might have distinguished them was their scent, but only if they wore different colognes, aftershaves, or shampoos. But they smelled just the same.

She didn't want Florence or her grandfather to help get rid of the bodies so she went to the window in the guest room she and Rory weren't using and opened it. "We need to dump them here."

"Right." Rory helped her move one of the bodies through the room, lifted him to the windowsill, and shoved him out. He fell into the snow and sank several feet.

When they went back to retrieve the other body, Frank and Florence were trying to move him. "We've got this," Rory said.

Lacy was glad that he didn't want them to help. She could see them putting their backs out of whack.

Then she and Rory carried the last body into the bedroom and tossed him out where he landed in the snow and, due to the softness, sank a couple of feet. The snow was still coming down and they would soon be buried completely, which worked for them.

"How did they get in?" Frank asked.

"They were in our guest room." Rory headed out of the other guest room and pulled the door open to their room.

Lacy expected the window to be broken, but it wasn't. She went over to the window and pulled it up. It wasn't locked. "When could they have unlocked it? Oh, damn, there's the trellis on top of the snow and next to the window. They moved it to the window and used it to navigate over the snow. But again all the windows were locked, weren't they?"

"They were," Florence said.

"But earlier they broke into the house and knocked the Christmas tree down a second time." Frank peered out the window at the trellis. "They could have gone upstairs and unlocked the window so they could return later without breaking it and alerting us."

"We had already smelled their scent in the guest room so we weren't alerted that they had been there again," Lacy said.

"Right. I'm just glad they didn't come through the window when we were sleeping," Rory said.

"No, they waited until after we were downstairs, probably until the light was off in the upstairs part of the house, indicating we had moved to the lower floor," Frank said.

At least Lacy was glad they were safe now from the threat.

THE NEXT MORNING, Florence woke to her phone's ringtone and picked up her phone from the bedside table. They had phone service!

Dan was calling.

"Hello, we finally have phone service! The brothers are dead."

"At the house?" Dan asked.

"In the mountain of snow out back," she said.

"The blizzard has stopped, snow has stopped. We're clearing the roads, and we'll be at your place before long. Is everyone safe?"

"We are. No one was injured in the fight."

"Okay, we'll retrieve the bodies when we're able. Tell Rory we're clearing the road to the ranch also. I guess now you don't need any more protection," Dan said.

"No, we're good. I'll be opening the coffee shop as soon as the roads are cleared."

"All right. See you later."

Frank was sitting up in bed. "Was that Dan?"

"Yeah, it sure was. The blizzard has stopped. I thought there was an eerie quietness."

"Yeah, we've been listening to that howling wind for so long, I didn't realize it had ceased." Frank climbed out of bed.

A knock on the door made them both jump a little. They smiled at each other. "Yes?" Florence called out.

"We've got cell service," Rory said. "Hal just called. The roads are still impassible, so he told me to stay here until they're cleared. I told him we got rid of the threat."

Florence and Frank had finished dressing, went to the door, and opened it. "Dan called and told us they're clearing the roads now, but that it will be a while before they reach the ranch," Florence said.

"Yeah, we figured that. The guys are using a couple of snow machines to clean up the parking area and the drive onto the ranch."

"I bet they're missing you." Lacy began making bacon and eggs.

Frank got the coffee, and Florence served orange juice to everyone. "How are you feeling, Rory?"

"Better already, just knowing the snow will be cleared away."

Then they heard snowplows, whooped and hollered, left their untouched breakfast on the dining room table, and looked out the front windows.

Two snowplows were moving snow off the main road. One reached Florence's driveway and began shoveling it.

"Yes!" Florence said. "I have a snowblower. Once the snowplow is gone, we can use it to clear the area next to the garage door, and then we'll clean off your truck."

"See? They're already ready for us to leave," Rory joked.

Everyone laughed.

"It will be a while before they clear the road all the way to the ranch," Florence said. "And we love having your company. This has been a real treat for us."

"I agree," Lacy said. "Except for Rory getting claustrophobic, it's been delightful."

Rory smiled and kissed Lacy. "For sure."

Then they all sat down to eat breakfast before donning their winter clothes and heading outside with ice and snow scrapers, the snowblower, and snow shovels.

Florence and Frank were using snow brushes to push the heavy snow off Rory's pickup while Rory was using the snowblower to clear a path on either side of the truck and in front of it where the snowplow couldn't go. Then he was working on the walkway to the front door and the front porch. Lacy scraped away the snow and ice on the windshield.

Dan, Stryker, Travis, Ricky, and Chase arrived to retrieve the brothers' bodies.

"What are you going to do with them?" Florence asked.

"How were they killed?" Dan asked.

"Cougar attack," Rory said.

"Cremation then. If anyone comes looking for them, they'll be gone. There will be no evidence that cougars killed them," Dan said. "We don't want to bury them out here. Their ashes will be dropped into one of the closed silver mines."

"We've got their guns. They're on the table in the hallway on the second floor. Do you want me to get them for you?" Frank asked.

"I'll get them." Rory went inside the house while the other men went out back to dig out the brothers' bodies.

They would have to patch up all the places where the bullets struck the walls and ceiling.

"What if someone comes looking for them? Friends or family?" Lacy asked. "Timothy never mentioned his twin brother or anyone else in the family. So I don't know if he has any. Though a friend or two might come looking for him. Even someone at the PI agency they were running."

"Does anyone know about you dating Timothy?" Dan asked.

"Only my grandfather. I don't know about anyone he might have told except his brother."

Rory returned with the guns. "Here they are. We'll have to get rid of their cars too."

"We will." Dan took the guns and put them in his vehicle.

Then he and Rory began helping to dig out the brothers from the snowdrift.

"I want to check on my coffee shop," Florence said.

Rory shoveled some more snow away from the house. "I'll take you. Are you going to open it up?"

"I might. Just in case townsfolk want coffee and pastries after being buried at home."

"I'll go with you and help out," Lacy said.

"I'll ask if Ava wants to join us. She doesn't have to, but she might feel a little housebound. We might not get much business though."

"I'll bring the snowblower and clean off the sidewalk in front of your coffee shop," Rory said.

"What can I do to help?" Frank asked, sounding a little left out.

"Greet customers if we have any?"

"I can do that."

Lacy and Florence watched the men carry the bodies to the ambulance that just pulled into the driveway. Once they were loaded into the ambulance, it left.

"Are you all right?" Dan asked them again.

"Yeah, we're going to the coffee shop and opening it up," Florence said.

"We'll drop by and pick up some things from your shop," Dan said.

Florence smiled. "Thanks. You may give us the only business we'll have."

Then Dan and the other guys left, and she locked up her house. Rory drove her, Lacy, and Frank in Rory's pickup to the coffee shop. He seemed really happy to be behind the wheel again and not hemmed in.

When they reached the shop, they found the snow piled high against the windows and door. The road and parking spots had been cleared, but they still needed to work on the sidewalk. Rory got started on it.

Once he cleared a pathway to the front door, Florence unlocked it, and she, Lacy, and Frank went into the shop.

Florence called Ava while Lacy started the coffee. "Hey, Ava, I opened the coffee shop. I'm not sure if we'll get anybody here so you don't need to come in if you don't want to. Lacy and Frank are here with me. Rory is out clearing the sidewalk with my snowblower."

"No customers?"

"No, and we didn't see anyone on the road either."

"Okay, I'm staying home with the kids then. I'll come in tomorrow."

"That's fine. I'll let you know if business picks up."

Rory was still clearing the sidewalk and finally put the snow-blower in the truck, then came in for some hot chocolate and to warm up. "It's done."

Just as he spoke, customers were beginning to venture out, probably feeling just as snowbound as they had been. When they saw Florence's shop was open, they began pulling into the parking lot.

"Looks like we're open for business," she said, thrilled they had come in to get things ready.

Frank finished his coffee and began bringing menus to everyone and getting them water.

"What a storm," one couple said. "We were at the motel and didn't think we would ever get out of there. The owners had to feed us until we could leave."

"I'm so glad the storm is over," Frank said. "Much longer, and we would all have gone a little stir crazy."

"I agree."

Then Frank took their orders and turned them over to Florence. She had just finished making the fresh soup and brought it to the table while Frank greeted Dan.

"Is everything taken care of?" Frank was referring to the brothers.

"Yeah. Done."

"Are you here to pick up something to eat?"

"Yeah. We need some hot sandwiches to go—beef brisket, if Florence has the meat for it."

"I sure do," Florence said. "I'll make them right away." She had already cooked the brisket and frozen it, so it wouldn't take long to reheat and grill the sandwiches. "How many do you need?"

"Seven. We're all coming in to eat and then head out to help anyone in need due to the blizzard."

"Coming right up." Florence and Lacy both worked together to make the sandwiches.

Then more people came into the shop, and Rory finished his cocoa and started taking orders too.

Florence and Lacy finished the sandwiches and bagged them, but when she left the kitchen to give them to Dan, a man came to the door, opened it, and walked inside. Her jaw dropped. Dan turned around to see who was at the door and saw the exact clone of Timothy and Manning that she saw.

"Are you the sheriff?" the man asked.

"Yeah, I am."

"I want to file a missing person's report for my brothers, Timothy and Manning Wrangler. Your dispatcher said you were here. My brothers came here looking for—"

Peering out of the kitchen to see what the problem was, Lacy dropped the knife she'd been using to cut up sandwiches, and it hit the floor with a clatter.

"Her!" the man said. "Where are they? Where are my brothers?" He sounded furious with Lacy for luring them to Yuma Town as if it were her fault that they had followed her there.

"How should I know? I broke it off with Timothy months ago, but nothing I said worked. He wouldn't take no for an answer. I left Orlando to get away from him. He followed me to New Orleans, then here." Lacy folded her arms. "I keep getting restraining orders to keep him away from me, but he ignores them. So who are you exactly?"

"Canton Wrangler. Timothy called me and said he followed you here, that some guy was making the moves on you."

Great. So this guy knew they had been there for sure.

"That would be me," Rory said, moving next to Lacy and taking her hand and squeezing it. "We're marrying soon."

If human customers hadn't been there enjoying a bite of food, Florence figured Rory would have said he was mated to Lacy.

"So where are my brothers?" Canton asked.

"How would I know?" Lacy asked. "They never came to the coffee shop. This is where I'm working now. I'm staying at a horse ranch. They never went there either."

Florence was glad that they hadn't come here, or Canton would be able to smell that the brothers, or at least one of them, had been there.

"You can file a missing persons' report at the office. I'll lead you there," Dan said to Canton.

"I want to talk further with her." Canton jerked a thumb at Lacy.

"She said she hasn't seen them." Dan's voice was much sterner now.

The other customers took that as a cue to finish their meals and leave the shop.

"I think she has seen them."

"Did they tell you that?" Dan asked.

"No. I lost contact with them, maybe because of the blizzard. Timothy only told me he had found her in Yuma Town, Colorado."

"A lot of people were stranded due to the storm," Dan agreed.

Though Dan had never said that anyone had been, so Florence thought he was making that up. The cougars living in Yuma Town and beyond had had fair warning and had probably stayed put when the storm hit, unless they were strictly humans and had been caught up in the blizzard.

15

R arely did humans or cougars have identical triplets. Lacy couldn't believe there was another brother who was the spitting image of Timothy and Manning. Canton wasn't listed as one of the PIs at the agency Timothy and Manning had been at. She wondered what he worked at.

Canton didn't seem to buy Dan's story. Maybe because he realized most of the people that he was meeting in Yuma Town were all cougars, and they could be protecting her.

She couldn't help that her heart was pounding like crazy, and she felt sick to her stomach. She had thought this business with Timothy and Manning was over. But she loved that Rory was standing by her side, comforting her and offering his support.

Dan said, "Your brothers were stalking Lacy. She came here trying to get away from them. We'll be glad to look for your missing brothers, but don't bother Lacy about this. She has already told you she hasn't seen them."

"All right." Canton gave Lacy a dirty look, as if she were the one responsible for all this.

Then he followed Dan out of the shop, and Lacy breathed a

sigh of relief. Rory hugged and kissed her. "If he tries to harass you at the ranch or anywhere, he'll meet the same end as his brothers."

She hugged him back, glad that he was her mate.

Lacy and Florence continued to make food for the customers while Rory and Frank delivered meals to the tables. They seemed to be all right with working at the coffee shop. She was surprised they were so busy, but suspected it was because everyone had been stuck at home for so long.

They had lunch there, and then when they were done at the end of the day, they headed to Florence's house to drop off Frank and Florence. They left off the snowblower. They didn't have any bags at Florence's house, just their Christmas presents, so they grabbed them and hugged and thanked them for a delightful Christmas. Then they drove to the ranch so Rory could get back to work.

"He's not going to bother you, Lacy. We'll all see to it," Rory said.

"What if Canton is as much of a bulldog as his brothers?" Lacy asked.

"He can look for them all he wants. No one will tell him what happened to them, and he won't find any clues. If he did go to Florence's house, he might be able to smell his brothers' scents on the outside, but he won't be allowed inside, and that will be the end of that," Dan said.

"Unless he breaks in like they did. And there are bullet holes all over the place upstairs in the hallway."

"If anything, since no one will tell him that you were staying with Florence, he might come out to the ranch. But he won't smell their scents around the ranch. By the waterfall, maybe. If the blizzard didn't get rid of them," Rory said.

Then Lacy got a call from Dan. "Hi, Dan, what's up?" She put the call on speakerphone.

"We found one of the brothers' cars. It was buried in the snow near Florence's house. We've impounded it and notified Canton so he can take a look. But it's in the impound yard, not by her home. We don't want him connecting the dots."

"He'll ask where you found it."

"We'll tell him near the motel. They had stayed there a night. They'd been wearing disguises. The owner didn't recognize them when they stayed there."

"Oh, that's awful. I mean that they were there, and none of us knew it. What about the other car?"

"We were going to turn it into scrap metal, but since Canton's here, he can make arrangements to take both home with him, if he wants."

"He's not going to leave, is he? Not before he finds his brothers."

"There are still two of them. They're quadruplets, all identical. The other is Ren. He says he wants to return home, that they are on a fool's errand. That they should never have come after their brothers. That they were wrong to go after you."

"At least one of the four of them has some sense."

"Let's hope he convinces Canton to go home with him and leave well enough alone. But they might leave the cars here in case Timothy and Manning show up."

If the men were close to each other, she didn't believe they would leave without finding their brothers. They wouldn't have come all the way there otherwise.

"They are cremated, right?" she asked.

"Yes, and down in the mine. So they'll never find them."

She sighed deeply. "All right. Oh, what about their cell phones and ID?"

"Destroyed, down in the mines with them. Hey, Ren's coming into the office. I'll let you go."

"All right, thanks, Dan."

She sat back in the passenger seat. "There are four of them— identical quadruplets."

"Ahh, hell," Rory said.

"I know. But at least the fourth brother, Ren, sounds more reasonable. He was against coming out here."

A few minutes later, Dan called back, and she put the call on speakerphone again. "Hey, Ren said he has convinced Canton to return to Florida with him. He said that they put in the missing persons' requests, and if we find them, to let them know. Otherwise, they would assume they came to a bad end in the storm, and they'll deal with that if it comes to that."

"So they're really leaving town then?" Rory asked. "Were you able to get Bridget to the sheriff's office to read their thoughts to see if they were being sincere?"

Lacy stared at Rory. One of the cougars could read thoughts?

"No. We didn't expect Ren to come in and tell me they're leaving."

"So what do we do about Lacy's safety?" Rory asked.

"I'm going to work at the coffee shop tomorrow." Lacy wasn't going to be stuck at the ranch now that Timothy and Manning were gone. She suspected that Ren was in charge of the remaining brother and would steer Canton on the right path.

"We're going to have some of our people surreptitiously follow them out for a few miles to make sure they're actually heading out of town," Dan said.

"Okay, good." Rory relaxed a little, then drove onto the ranch. "We're just now arriving home."

"Have a good night. Talk to you later," Dan said, and they said goodnight, and they ended the call.

"Bridget?" Lacy asked.

"Travis's mate is also a CSF special agent," Rory said. "She's able to read minds."

"Wow. That must come in handy in her line of work. Do you have any other psychics in town other than Nina and Ava, also?"

"Well, if you hadn't heard, Chase, Stryker, and Leyton have seen ghosts before. Chase, more so than the others, when they were on a mission in a ghost town."

"That's amazing." Then she bit her lip. "Did any of them see the brothers' ghosts?"

Rory got on his Bluetooth and called Chase. "Hey, Lacy wants to know if you saw the brothers' ghosts when you were retrieving their bodies from the mountain of snow."

"No. I don't always see them, thank heavens," Chase said. "I asked Leyton and Stryker if they had just out of curiosity's sake, but they both said they hadn't."

"Good. So they're not hanging about Florence's home to haunt her or me when I visit."

"Right. Just to let you know, some of us are following Ren and Canton out of town to ensure they're leaving for good," Chase said.

"Oh, that's great. What is Dan going to do about Timothy and Manning's cars?" she asked.

"Leave them in case they show up looking for them," Chase said. "We'll let them know if we don't find the 'missing' brothers after so long, and they can decide what to do with their vehicles."

"I don't think Canton believed me when I said I hadn't seen the brothers."

"Yeah. I wish Bridget could have been there to overhear the conversation. They're pulling off the road for gas, so I need to let you go."

"All right. Thanks, Chase."

"No problem. We keep our own people safe."

She and Rory left the truck and headed inside the bunkhouse, but before they could remove their coats and boots and slip off to their bedroom, Blaze and Wyatt began harassing Rory for taking an extended holiday vacation.

Rory just smiled. "We needed the extra time for each other."

"Are the two of you all right?" Wyatt asked, all joking aside.

"Yeah." Lacy explained about the men being identical quadruplets, but that the other two had left town.

Blaze rubbed his beard, frowning. "Were you able to tell them apart?"

"We only saw one of them, but he looked identical to Timothy and Manning. They smelled the same, talked the same, just identical in all ways," she said.

"That had to be a shock when you saw the new one," Wyatt said.

"It was. I nearly fainted. If I had seen both of them, I would have thought that Timothy and Manning had come back from the dead."

"Yeah, I think all of us felt that way," Rory said. "I hope your Christmas was good."

His friends grunted at him. "It was, until we had to navigate the snow to feed the animals without an extra ranch hand," Wyatt said.

Rory smiled. "I knew you could do it."

"If you must know," Lacy said, rubbing Rory's back, "he really worried about you guys doing all that work and about the animals."

"Ted and Hal were out helping us," Blaze said. "You know how they are. There's no job too big or small that they won't help out when they're needed."

"Well, we're pooped. We're going to hit the shower and go to bed," Wyatt said. "We're glad you got rid of the menace, and you're back home safely. All the reception was out here, and we tried to check on you, worried you might try and make it back home to work."

"We couldn't. The road conditions were just too bad." Rory showed them the picture he took of the wall of snow at the garage door.

"Damn. We were glad you stayed with Florence and Frank," Blaze said.

THEN THEY ALL retired for the night, and the next morning, Lacy got ready to go to work. Rory was already out doing ranch work, but before she left, he kissed her. "Are you sure you're going to be all right on your own?"

"Yes, I feel great. No blizzard, no more brothers to harass me, no more need for protection."

He hugged and kissed her. "All right. I'll see you for dinner."

"See you, honey." She was ready to get back to a regular routine, even though she had just started working there.

She drove off, glad the roads were pretty clear. They were still packed with snow, but perfectly drivable. She called Florence on Bluetooth. "Hey, Grandma." She thought she would try calling Florence her grandmother.

Florence laughed. "That sounds great. Are you coming in, or are the roads too bad?"

"I'm coming in. I'm about..."

Suddenly, a truck started to veer out of his lane and headed straight for her. A drunk driver? She didn't have anywhere to go but into the snowbanks created by the snowplows.

She lay on the horn, but the truck was fully in her lane and getting close.

"What's wrong?" Florence asked, sounding worried. Then she said, "Ava, call Dan. Lacy's on the way here again, but she's in trouble on the road."

Lacy tried swerving into the truck's lane to get out of his path, but he corrected his driving, targeting her. "Pickup coming from Yuma Town," she hurriedly told Florence. "He's aiming his truck right at me."

He struck her car hard, she screamed, and drove into the snowbank.

Then she was stuck. She tried to back out, but her front wheels were too deep in the snow. His truck had a big bumper grill to protect it, but hers was badly smashed.

"He has got a gun."

"Stay in the car. Ava's calling Dan and Rory. Everyone's headed your way."

"It's one of the quadruplet brothers."

"Letting everyone know."

"Get out of the car!" the brother yelled at her.

She didn't respond. She was scared to pieces, and she wasn't getting out of the car where he could take her somewhere else and kill her.

"You know what happened to them! Get. Out. Of. The. Car. Now."

"What do you want? And which one are you?" She suspected it was Canton, that he would force the truth out of her.

"Canton, but I suspect you know that. Ren didn't want any part of this, so he returned to Florida. Me? I'm going to learn the truth, and you're going to tell me."

"Ren didn't believe what Timothy and Manning were doing was right."

"I don't give a damn about you. I just want to know where my brothers are."

"I told you. I never saw them at the shop. You would have smelled them if they had been there. And the same with the ranch. But I'm sure they would have realized they couldn't have hassled me there, not with all the ranch hands who work there. Then the blizzard came, and who knows what happened to them."

"They would have shifted to stay warm. They didn't stay in their cars."

"Then look for them. I'm not leaving the car."

"The sheriff's office isn't looking for them, are they?"

No, they're looking for Canton though.

Then she heard cars and trucks tearing down the road, coming from both directions, converging on Canton's truck and her car. Lights and sirens were going.

She wanted to open her door and slam it against him to make him drop the gun in the piled-up snow. He raised the gun and pointed it at her. "Maybe you don't know where they are, but if they're dead because of you, you're going to pay for it."

She didn't have a choice. No one was there yet, and if he shot her, she would be dead. She unlocked the door and slammed it against him, and the round he had chambered went overhead.

She closed the door and locked it. Rory's truck came sailing from behind, veered off, and struck Canton hard, knocking him into the snow.

The other vehicles rushed up to join them. Rory jumped out of his truck in a heartbeat. He immediately plowed through the snow to reach Canton and made sure he couldn't harm anyone. She got out of her car and joined him.

"Is he..."

"Dead. Where's the other one?" Rory stood and wrapped his arms around her.

"Going home. Ren didn't want to be involved in this any longer."

"Smart man."

Dan, Chase, Stryker, Leyton, Ricky, and Travis exited their vehicles at a run. So did Hal, Ted, Wyatt, and Blaze. They all surrounded them, and Dan checked out Canton, shaking his head. "It's Canton, right?"

"Yeah. He said Ren returned home," Lacy said, clinging to Rory.

"I'll notify Ren that his brother is dead after he pulled a gun on you. Hopefully, he'll understand what was at stake," Dan said.

"Good." She was glad that he would know what happened to the one brother and could probably presume that his other brothers met a similar fate.

"You're coming home, right?" Rory asked Lacy.

RORY WANTED her home with him. But he would support her if she wanted to go to work. He would take her, though.

"Yeah, I think I'll skip work today," she said.

"We'll have your car towed and fixed up," Dan said. "And we'll take care of Canton and his truck."

She got a call from Florence, answered it, and put it on speakerphone.

"Are you all right?" Florence asked.

"Yes, thanks. You sent reinforcements, and they rescued me."

"Oh, I'm so glad. Why don't you take a day off from work?" Florence asked.

"You're all right with it?"

"If I were you, I would do it. Frank is home while someone is over there filling all the bullet holes in the upstairs hallway and painting them after that, and Ava is here with me, helping out with the coffee shop. I want you to relax after what you've been through."

"Thanks, uh, Grandma."

Florence chuckled. "I love it when you call me that. I feel like I have a family again."

"You do."

THEN THEY ENDED THE CALL, and Rory drove Lacy back to the ranch. "Thanks for my rescue."

"I was just glad I got there before it was too late." He couldn't afford to lose her ever.

"Me too." She sighed. "Our new year will be the best ever."

"I agree." With no more trouble from the Wranglers, it would be. He was so glad Lacy had come into his life. He couldn't believe how much trouble she'd been in until the brothers came after her. "We have a New Year's dance coming up."

"And a wonderful dance partner to enjoy it with. You are my everything."

"Mine too." And he couldn't wait to marry her and go on their honeymoon. But for now, he was just glad to take her home and keep her safe.

EPILOGUE

After a wonderful New Year's dance where Florence and Frank danced until the fireworks went off to welcome in the new year, and so did Lacy and Rory and all the other partygoers, they were ready to get married and then head out on their honeymoons.

Six months later, Hal gave Lacy away at the wedding, and Dan gave Florence away. They loved it. But at the banquet, a rumor was spreading that Ted and Stella were pregnant with twins. And even though it was a wedding celebration for two couples, Lacy and Rory, and Florence and Frank toasted to Stella and Ted's upcoming babies that would join the cougars of Yuma Town.

Ted and Stella were smiling broadly and thanking them for announcing their special news at the wedding celebratory dinner.

Then the newly married couples were off on their honeymoons. Florence and Frank flew to Portland, Oregon, and rented a car to drive to their cabin retreat on the Oregon Coast, while Lacy and Rory flew to Belize. Both couples were staying near the water, but Lacy and Rory planned to do a lot of snorkeling in Belize. In contrast, Florence and Frank intended to do a lot of walking along the beach, both as cougars and humans. They also took boat trips to see whales and porpoises. The red wolves on the Oregon Coast treated them to a hamburger cookout and even ran with them in their shifter forms.

They were delighted to meet cougar shifters.

Frank and Florence really enjoyed the company, but the cabin was great for their special alone time too, and they loved listening to the ocean waves crashing on the shore. They even saw a black bear and two cougars, non-shifter types, while they were running at night.

"I never thought I would be on my honeymoon at a red wolf-owned cabin rental with a fellow FBI agent," Florence said, sitting on the deck with Frank, sharing champagne, wrapped in blankets together on a rocking bench.

Frank leaned over and kissed her. "I'm so glad you picked this spot for us. It is the perfect getaway for the two of us. And so many of the red wolf pack have come out to meet us, it feels like we're celebrities."

"I wonder how the kids are doing," Florence said.

"Oh, you know they're having fun—running through the rainforest, enjoying the beaches and clear, aqua water. But this place is perfect for us."

"Are you ready to go back inside and get warmed up?"

Frank helped her up from the bench. "You betcha."

Lacy and Rory spent a lot of time in the Belize rainforest on night excursions and were surprised to see as many wild cats as they did: full-time cougars, jaguars, ocelots, jaguarundis, and margays.

But for now, they were just finishing snorkeling at one of the reefs and headed back to their car so they could return to their cabin in the rainforest. "Are you ready for a swim in the pool?" Lacy asked.

Rory laughed. "I didn't know you were part mermaid."

"I was born and raised in Florida, remember?"

"Aww. I love it. I love you."

They washed off, headed to the indoor swimming pool, which was happily empty, and swam. Then they were hugging in the water. It wasn't long before Rory wanted to take this somewhere more private.

"Are you ready to retire to the cabin?" Rory asked.

"Yeah, I can feel you're ready for me. Let's go."

"I wonder how Frank and Florence are doing." Rory opened the door for her, and they went inside and locked it.

"Having as much fun as us, I'm sure." Though she suspected they weren't in bed half as much as Rory and she had been for another wild romp!

Then again, what did she know?

ACKNOWLEDGMENTS

To Darla Taylor and Donna Fournier, who spotted the flaws I couldn't see and nudged me toward better versions with kindness at every turn. Your commitment made this a far better book than it would have been without you.

ABOUT THE AUTHOR

USA Today bestselling and award-winning author **Terry Spear** has written over a hundred paranormal romance novels, young adult, and medieval Highland historical romances. Her first werewolf romance, *Heart of the Wolf,* was named a 2008 *Publishers Weekly*'s Best Book of the Year, and her subsequent titles have garnered high praise and hit the *USA Today* bestseller list. A retired officer of the U.S. Army Reserves, Terry lives in Spring, Texas, where she is working on her next werewolf romance, shapeshifting jaguars, cougar shifters, vampires, hot Highlanders, and having fun with her young adult fae and vampire novels, helping with her grandchildren and raising two Havanese.

For more information, please visit her website at: http://www.terryspear.com

Blog: https://terryspearbooks.blog/

Follow her for new releases and book deals: www.bookbub.com/authors/terry-spear

Twitter: @TerrySpear.

Facebook: http://www.facebook.com/terry.spear

ALSO BY TERRY SPEAR

Adult Titles

Romantic Suspense: Deadly Fortunes, In the Dead of the Night, Relative Danger, Bound by Danger

***

The Highlanders Series: His Wild Highland Lass (novella), Vexing the Highlander (novella), Winning the Highlander's Heart, The Accidental Highland Hero, Highland Rake, Taming the Wild Highlander, The Highlander, Her Highland Hero, The Viking's Highland Lass, My Highlander, Stolen Highland Dreams

Other historical romances: Lady Caroline & the Egotistical Earl, A Ghost of a Chance at Love

***

Heart of the Wolf Series: Heart of the Wolf, Destiny of the Wolf, To Tempt the Wolf, Legend of the White Wolf, Seduced by the Wolf, Wolf Fever, Heart of the Highland Wolf, Dreaming of the Wolf, A SEAL in Wolf's Clothing, A Howl for a Highlander, A Highland Werewolf Wedding, A SEAL Wolf Christmas, Silence of the Wolf, Hero of a Highland Wolf, A Highland Wolf Christmas; SEAL Wolf Hunting; A Silver Wolf Christmas, SEAL Wolf in Too Deep, Alpha Wolf Need Not Apply, Between a Wolf and a Hard Place, SEAL Wolf Undercover, Dreaming of a White Wolf Christmas, Flight of the White Wolf, All's Fair in Love and Wolf, A Billionaire Wolf for Christmas, SEAL Wolf Surrender, Silver Town Wolf: Home for the Holidays, Night of the Billionaire Wolf, You Had Me at Wolf, Joy to the Wolves, The Wolf Wore Plaid, Jingle Bell Wolf, The Best of Both Wolves, While the Wolf's Away, Christmas Wolf Surprise, Wolf Takes the Lead, Wolf on the Wild Side, Her Wolf for the Holidays, A Good Wolf is

Hard to Find (2024), Dreaming of a Highland Wolf (2024), Wolf Bound, Mated for Christmas (2024) , The Wolf of My Eye

SEAL Wolves: To Tempt the Wolf, A SEAL in Wolf's Clothing, A SEAL Wolf Christmas; SEAL Wolf Hunting, A SEAL Wolf in Too Deep, SEAL Wolf Undercover, SEAL Wolf Surrender

Silver Town Wolves: Destiny of the Wolf, Wolf Fever, Dreaming of the Wolf, Silence of the Wolf; A Silver Wolf Christmas, Between a Wolf and a Hard Place, Home for the Holidays, Jingle Bell Wolf

Wolff Family Lodge Wolves: You Had Me at Wolf, Wolf on the Wild Side, A Good Wolf is Hard to Find

Highland Wolves: Heart of the Highland Wolf, A Howl for a Highlander, A Highland Werewolf Wedding, Hero of a Highland Wolf, A Highland Wolf Christmas, The Wolf Wore Plaid, Her Wolf for the Holidays, Dreaming of a Highland Wolf, The Wolf of My Eye

Billionaire Wolf Series: A Billionaire in Wolf's Clothing, A Billionaire Wolf for Christmas, Night of the Billionaire Wolf, Wolf Takes the Lead

White Wolf Series: Legend of the White Wolf, Dreaming of a White Wolf Christmas, Flight of the White Wolf, While the Wolf's Away, Mated for Christmas

Red Wolf Series: Seduced by the Wolf, Joy to the Wolves, The Best of Both Wolves, Christmas Wolf Surprise

Greystoke Wolf Pack: Wolf Bound,

Wolf Novellas: Day of the Wolf, Seal Wolf Pursuit, Wolf to the Rescue, Night of the Wolf, United Shifter Force, Wolfish

***

Heart of the Jaguar Series: Savage Hunger, Jaguar Fever, Jaguar Hunt, Jaguar Pride, A Very Jaguar Christmas, You Had Me at Jaguar, The Witch and the Jaguar, Dawn of the Jaguar

***

Heart of the Cougar Series: Cougar's Mate, Call of the Cougar, Taming the Wild Cougar, Covert Cougar Christmas, a novella, Double Cougar Trouble, Cougar Undercover, Cougar Magic, Cougar Halloween Mischief, Falling for the Cougar, Cougar Christmas Calamity, Catch the Cougar (Halloween Novella), You Had Me at Cougar, Saving the White Cougar, Big Cat Magic

***

White Bear Series: Loving the White Bear, Claiming the White Bear, Bear of a Halloween, Protecting the White Bear

Grizzly Bear Series: Bear in Mind

***

Highland Wolves of Old: Wolf Pack, Wolf Alliance, Wolf Heir

Heart of the Huntress Series: Killing the Bloodlust, Deadly Liaisons, Huntress for Hire, Forbidden Love, Deadly Liaisons, Vampire Redemption, Primal Desire, Huntress Unleashed

Vampire Novellas: The Siren's Lure, Vampiric Calling, Seducing the Huntress

***

Comedy Romance: Exchanging Grooms, Marriage, Las Vegas Style

***

Science Fiction: Galaxy Warrior

Young Adult Titles

The World of Fae:

The Dark Fae

The Deadly Fae

The Winged Fae

The Ancient Fae

Dragon Fae

Hawk Fae

Phantom Fae

Golden Fae

Falcon Fae

Woodland Fae

Angel Fae

***

The World of Elf:

The Shadow Elf

The Darkland Elf

Warrior Elf

***

Blood Moon Series:

Kiss of the Vampire

Bite of the Vampire

Night of the Vampire

The Vampire Chronicles Series:

The Vampire in My Dreams

Demon Guardian Series:

The Trouble with Demons

Demon Trouble, Too

Demon Hunter

Non-Series for Now:

Ghostly Liaisons

The Beast Within

Courtly Masquerade

Deidre's Secret

The Magic of Inherian:

The Scepter of Salvation

The Mage of Monrovia

Emerald Isle of Mists

Tashama